W9-CMH-089

Faraway Summer

By Johanna Hurwitz

JOHANNA HURWITZ

Faraway Summer

Illustrated by Mary Azarian

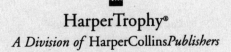

HarperTrophy®
A Division of HarperCollinsPublishers

HarperTrophy® is a registered trademark of HarperCollins Publishers Inc.

Faraway Summer
Text copyright © 1998 by Johanna Hurwitz
Illustrations copyright © 1998 by Mary Azarian

All rights reserved. No part of this book may be reproduced in any
manner whatsoever without written permission except in the case of
brief quotations embodied in critical articles or reviews.
Printed in the United States of America.
For information address HarperCollins Children's Books, a division of
HarperCollins Publishers, 1350 Avenue of the Americas, New York, NY 10019.

Library of Congress Cataloging-in-Publication Data
Hurwitz, Johanna.
    Faraway summer / by Johanna Hurwitz; illustrated by Mary Azarian.
        p.   cm.
    Summary: In the summer of 1910, Dossi, a poor Russian immigrant from the
tenements of New York, spends two weeks with the Meade family on their
Vermont farm, and all their lives are enriched by the experience.
    ISBN 0-688-15334-8—ISBN 0-380-73256-4 (pbk.)
    [1. Farm life—Vermont—Fiction.   2. Family life—Vermont—Fiction.
3. Jews—New York (N.Y.)—Fiction.   4. City and town life—Fiction.
5. Vermont—Fiction.]   I. Azarian, Mary, ill.   II. Title.
[PZ7.H9574Far   1998]   97-36363
[Fic]—dc21   CIP
                                                                        AC

First HarperTrophy edition, 2000

Visit us on the World Wide Web!
www.harperchildrens.com

For Alice Bayles, Judy & Joe Davison,
Gale Griffin, and all my other Vermont friends,
north, south, east, and west

Faraway Summer

July 30, 1910

My valise is almost packed. Tomorrow I'm leaving for two weeks in a place called Jericho. It's in the northern part of the state of Vermont. I'll be staying on a farm, so life there will be very different from what I know here in New York City. If I were going to the biblical town with the same name, it could not seem more faraway.

When Ruthi said that she had filled out an application to the Fresh Air Fund for me, I thought she was joking. How could my sister do such a thing without asking me? I'm not an infant. I'm twelve years old, almost thirteen! But ever since Mama died last year, Ruthi has acted as if there were sixteen years' difference in our ages and not just six.

"Oh, Dossi, it will be a wonderful experience," she insisted. "The fund was set up to send young people like you away from the city and the dirt and the crowds and the heat. You'll have a fine time in the country, breathing pure air and eating wholesome foods." Then she added, "You'll learn about country life and make new friends. You may not even want to come home again."

I truly doubt that. In fact, I was and still am very frightened of what is ahead of me. But once Ruthi has made up her mind, it's impossible to change it.

"You said, as soon as school was out for the summer, you'd arrange to get me a *real* job," I reminded her. I often help our landlady, Mrs. Aronson, take care of her children, but that work doesn't put any money in our pockets. However, Mrs. Aronson says she charges us less rent than she would someone else, because of my help.

"I never promised," Ruthi said. "Money is important, but we're managing with what I earn. You're too young and too smart to stay locked up inside a factory all day or sewing piecework at home. I want you to make good use of your time. Read books. Study. Perhaps your future can be brighter. Besides, you deserve a holiday from the Aronson children."

I think the real reason Ruthi wants me to go away is that she worries about my health. She's afraid I may have the same weaknesses in my body as our papa, who died of consumption. Papa was a scholar. He read many books before he came to America. Then he had to work too many hours, and his health got worse and worse. It's true that I'm like Papa in many ways. I have his interest in books and learning, and I've inherited his blue eyes and red hair. But Ruthi shouldn't worry so much about my health.

As soon as the letter came from the Fresh Air Fund saying that a place had been found for me, Ruthi started going through my clothing. Even though she spends twelve hours a day sewing at the Triangle Shirtwaist Factory, she began mending and patching all my clothes. Somehow she found the money to buy me a bathing costume.

"I'll never wear it," I told her when I saw the bloomers. They looked so foolish! Anyone seeing me wearing them would have a laughing fit. "I'll never go into any water beyond my ankles. And for that I can just lift up my skirts."

"It's best to be prepared," Ruthi insisted.

It appeared for a few days this week that I might not go away after all. There has been a strike of the railway workers, and we thought there might not be any trains running. The strange thing is that I was relieved and disappointed at the same time. But today we learned it is the freight trains that have been most affected by the strikers, and although there are some delays, passenger trains are going through.

So now my clothing is packed and ready for tomorrow. I've added a few little things to make me feel more at home when I arrive in Jericho. I put in the family portrait of Papa, Mama, little Velvel, Ruthi, and me. It was taken when we still lived in Russia. I don't remember posing, but Ruthi says I was afraid of the man with the big black camera. The picture lacks color, but when I look at it, I can imagine Papa's red beard and the feel of Mama's arm around my shoulder.

Papa went off to America soon after the picture was taken. It was three years until he earned enough money to send for the rest of us. By then I had almost forgotten Papa, and Velvel was dead from scarlet fever.

Now both Papa and Mama are gone too, and there are only Ruthi and me and the photograph left. Ruth and Hadassah Rabinowitz. Ruthi and Dossi.

In the midst of my packing I wished I had a good book to read during my trip. So I left my things and went off to the free lending library and borrowed two new books. My friend Miriam Sosnov came with me. How I wish she were coming with me to Jericho! "Don't tell the librarian that I'm going to take my library books to Vermont," I whispered to Mimi before we entered the library building. "Perhaps it's against the regulations. If I don't ask, she can't forbid me. And when I come back in two weeks, I'll return the books at once." The books will be three days late, but it will be worth sacrificing some penny candy to pay the library fine.

"This is a brand-new copy. You're the first person to borrow it," the librarian said, pointing to one of the books I had selected. It is *Anne of Green Gables,* by L. M. Montgomery. I don't know if L. M. is a man or a woman, but the book looks interesting.

"Take especially good care of it," the librarian warned me.

"I always take good care of the books," I said, wondering if she guessed that the book was about to go on a long train ride with me.

"Let me see your hands," she demanded. "Are they clean?"

Luckily I had remembered to wash them before leaving for the library.

"All right," she said.

I took my books, and Mimi and I rushed out the door before the librarian could ask me any more questions. We giggled together all the way home at my close escape. "Let me see your hands!" Mimi kept repeating, imitating the librarian's tone of voice. Now the books are safely inside my valise.

I've also packed my autograph album from school with all the messages and signatures of my classmates. They will keep me company among all the strangers I'll be meeting. And finally, when I finish writing tonight, I shall put in this new book of blank pages. Miss Blythe gave it to me as a prize for the best achievement in our seventh-grade class.

"You love to read other people's tales. Use this to write your own story," she had instructed me. And now I shall.

When Ruthi realized that I was going to pack my bottle of ink and my pen, she began to scold. "The ink will spill on all of your clothing. You'll look terrible!"

"I'd rather risk being covered with ink than leave it behind," I told her sharply. But then I remembered the library books. "I'll close the ink bottle very tightly and then wrap it inside the undergarments I've packed. That way, if it spills, no one will know about the blue stains but me," I told her.

Ruthi made a face, imagining me in inky underclothes, but she didn't say anything.

"Will you miss me?" I asked.

"Dossi, that's a foolish question."

"Yes, but you still haven't answered," I reminded her.

She stood for a moment looking at me. Then she began rubbing her eyes, which are always tired after her long hours of work. I realized all at once that there were tears in them. I threw my arms around her. "I'll miss you. But I'll write and tell you all about it."

"Don't spend all your money on postage stamps," she said, sniffing back her tears.

"You've given me fifty cents. That will be enough for many stamps, and candy and lemonades too."

"All right," she said. "Send me a card when you arrive so I know you made the journey safely."

"I'll find one with a beautiful picture," I promised.

So now I'm about to close my ink bottle

and close this journal. The next time I write, I won't be on Essex Street. I will be faraway in the land of Jericho. Can you blame me if I am tingling inside with both excitement and fright?

Reflections, A picturesque Vermont Landscape near St. Johnsbury

August 1, 1910

Dear Ruthi,

I'm safe and well. Vermont is another world from New York. I've never seen so much green— trees, fields, and mountains. The train ride is long but fascinating. I looked from my window for hours until it grew too dark. I also read and studied the other passengers before I fell asleep. Sleeping sitting up wasn't so bad. But I'm glad we have a bed at home. I wish you could be here with me.

Your affectionate sister,

Dossi

August 1, 1910

The train stopped for twenty minutes when we reached Rutland, Vermont. Many people got off to stretch their legs and to buy food from the vendors along the tracks who were selling fruit and sandwiches. There were a few railroad men with picket signs, but they didn't bother us.

Some people, like me, had to change trains. I took my valise and climbed down the steps of the train. It felt good to move about after sitting for so long. As I crossed the platform to board my connecting train, I almost bought an apple. I had eaten the bread and cheese and all four of the bruised peaches that Ruthi had packed up for me.

Then I saw a woman selling picture postcards. When I noticed the colorful scenes of Vermont, I remembered my promise to Ruthi. I took my pennies and, instead of buying a piece of fruit, I selected a card for my sister. I couldn't find a picture of Jericho, but the one I bought was hand-tinted, showing a picturesque landscape: a lake surrounded by large green trees. I bought a card with a different scene to send to Mimi, but I shall save it to post after I have been here a few days.

When I pasted the green penny stamp with Benjamin Franklin's face on the card for Ruthi, I envied it. I had bought the stamp at the post office near Essex Street before I left home. Soon it would journey back to the area from which it had come. If only I could be back home too. My hours on the train were enough to feed my thoughts for weeks to come. I did not need more adventure than that.

I had a double seat to myself the entire ride. I was relieved that I didn't have to sit shoulder to shoulder with a stranger for so many hours. Still, I found myself as fascinated by the other passengers as I was by the views from the train window. Where was everyone going? It was interesting to make up stories about each one. I couldn't help wondering if any of them were making up a story about me, a twelve-year-old girl traveling alone.

A beautifully dressed older woman was traveling alone too. I thought she looked rather sad and guessed there had been a tragedy in her life. There were several men who smoked and read newspapers. One of the men snored so loudly when he fell asleep that I almost burst out laughing. I also saw a young woman about Ruthi's age traveling with a young man. They held hands and whispered to each other all the time. Perhaps they were newly married, for they seemed so pleased to be sitting together on the train.

There was so much I wanted to tell Ruthi and Mimi, but there is too little room on a postcard even to begin. Two weeks are not so long, I reminded myself. Soon I would be going back home again, and I would tell them both every little detail about my trip.

The journey to Vermont went on and on and on. I thought it would never end. At the same time I knew that every moment I was getting closer to my destination, and I felt more and more nervous. I worried about the family with whom I was to stay. What kind of people would invite a stranger to move into their home and into their lives for two weeks? Would they like me? And even more important, would I like them?

They were waiting for me at the train station, holding a paper with my name on it. The peculiar thing is that the train stop was called Essex Junction. From Essex Street to Essex Junction. If I hadn't been so nervous, I would have smiled at the coincidence.

Waiting for me were Mr. and Mrs. Meade and their daughters, Emma and Eleanor. Even without having ever seen them before, I could tell they had on their best clothing to greet me.

I wished I were wearing something finer than my old skirt and blouse, but it is the best I own.

Emma Meade is fourteen, and Eleanor, who is called Nell, is almost nine years old. Both girls have long dark hair that they wear in braids. "Your age fits right in the middle between my girls," said Mrs. Meade, smiling at me.

Soon Nell began to chatter away. She had a hundred things she wanted to ask me and another hundred to tell. I noticed in her conversation that she, and the others too, use some expressions that seem funny to me. I'm going to try to remember everything so I can record their exact words.

"Do you know Mary Wells?" Nell asked me almost at once.

I shook my head. The name meant nothing to me.

"I was sure you would. Mary Wells lives in New York City too. She was here and stayed with the Bentley family in July. She's gone home now," Nell explained.

"There are thousands and thousands of people in New York," Emma told her sister in an exasperated tone. "Of course Hadassah won't know Mary. It isn't like Jericho, where we know everyone and everyone knows us."

"What kind of a name is Hadassah?" asked Mrs. Meade. "I've never heard it before. And I've never seen it on any of the stones in the graveyard either."

"I know two other Hadassahs in New York," I said, turning red. Those were the very first words that came out of my mouth to the family. Ruthi would have wanted me to thank the Meades for inviting me into their home. She would have wanted me to say how happy I was to be visiting them. But at that moment I wasn't feeling happy at all. I was feeling uncomfortable surrounded by so many strangers, so I didn't say those polite words.

"Hadassah must be a New York name," Nell said. She took my hand and pulled me toward their wagon.

"It's in the Bible," I told them. Mrs. Meade looked pleased when I said that.

I looked at the big animal attached to the

wagon. "Does this horse belong to your family?" I asked.

"Oh, yes. This is Dandy," said Nell, patting the horse on its nose. "We have one horse and six cows and a hog, fifteen chickens, and two barn cats," she announced proudly.

I couldn't believe my ears. I knew that the Meade family lived on a farm, but still it seemed to me it must be very crowded with so many animals. And the Meades must be very, very rich.

"You'll see many horses and cows as we ride home," Mrs. Meade told me. "Have you ever seen a horse this close up before?"

"I see hundreds of horses in New York," I told her. "Even though there seem to be more automobiles every day of the week, most of the merchants still use horses to pull their wares. There's the iceman and the milkman and the old-rags man and the man who sells vegetables."

Nell sat on one side of me, and Emma sat on the other. "You must be thirsty," said Mrs. Meade. She held out a large jar filled with liquid. "I put chips of ice in it, but they've all melted by now. Still, it's wet."

I took a little sip from the mouth of the jar. It had a sour-sweet taste that was not unpleasant and felt good going down my throat. "Now me," said Nell, grabbing at the jar. We passed it around, and everyone took a turn.

"Switchel is good on a hot day," said Mrs. Meade when she took the jar. I guessed that was what we were drinking.

"Is that a kind of fruit?" I asked. "A switchel?"

Nell let out a whoop of laughter. I blushed again. What had I said that was so funny?

"Switchel is made out of cider vinegar and molasses and water and a bit of powdered ginger," said Mrs. Meade. "We drink it often during hot weather."

"Cider vinegar comes from apples," said Nell. "Maybe we should call apples switchels from now on."

As we rode along, Nell kept busy explaining things to me. There are two more members of the family, sons aged eighteen and sixteen: Edward and Timothy. "They're both back home working in the fields," Nell explained. "And the cows need to be milked on time too."

"Nell, you're as noisy as a woodpecker," Emma complained as we rode along.

I didn't enjoy the wagon ride very much. Unlike the smooth motion of the train, we were bounced about in our seats so much that I worried I might fall out. The Vermont roads aren't paved the way streets are in New York. On one big bounce I accidentally bit my tongue. It hurt. A fine dust was stirred up too as we drove along, and it got into my eyes and nose. Before long my eyes were tearing, and I started to cough as well. What would Ruthi have to say about fresh air now? I wondered.

Still, I had to marvel at the enormous fields of dark green that we passed. I'd never seen or imagined anything like them before. Rows and rows and rows of plants bending with the wind.

"That's corn," said Nell when she saw me staring.

"It's enough corn to feed all of New York City," I observed with wonder.

"Not quite," Mr. Meade called over his shoulder to me. I think those were the only words he said to me or anyone on our journey. He's a very quiet man with a huge mustache.

"The corn is just about ready for picking," said his wife. "You'll get to eat a fair share before you leave here."

We also passed many fields full of cows. I saw horses and sheep as well.

"The cows are lying down. That means it's going to rain," Nell explained to me.

"Really?" I asked. "Maybe they're just tired."

"Cows don't get tired," said Nell, giggling.

The sun was shining, so I couldn't believe the cows knew that much about weather.

The houses along the way looked as if they had come out of my storybooks. Most were painted white and looked so clean. There were stretches of land between houses, not like New York, where we live on top of one another. It was all so different from home. Yet at the same time I saw clothing flapping in the breeze on wash lines, just like back on Essex Street. Even in Vermont people have laundry, I thought.

Another thing I noticed were the stone walls dividing the land.

"Each of those big stones was unearthed by farmers plowing the fields around here," Mrs. Meade explained when I commented on them. She pointed out how they were balanced on one another. "There's no mortar holding them together. There's an art to making a solid stone wall," she said.

"My brother Timothy can make them real good," Nell told me.

Finally we reached the Meades' home. It is huge. Everyone in our tenement could live in it and there would still be room for all the other people up and down our street. Emma and Nell share a bedroom at the top of the house. Next to it is a small room filled with trunks and boxes with still another bed, in the corner, for me. Imagine, there is a room just for eating meals. It has a long table and many chairs. Wouldn't the Meades be amazed to know that Ruthi and I cook and eat our meals and sleep all in the same room?

Nell showed me where the privy was, out behind the house in a tiny house of its own. It's just for their use. They don't have to share it with other families as Ruthi and I do. On the other hand, I imagine it must be pretty cold to go outdoors to do their business in the middle of the winter!

In the kitchen I washed my hands and face. I had to work a little pump in the sink to make the water flow. If you move it up and down, water comes out. Mrs. Meade told me that the water is from their own well. I smoothed back my hair and hoped that my appearance wouldn't have shamed Ruthi if she'd been there to see me. Then I was ready to join the family around the dinner table.

Mr. Meade lowered his head and folded his hands. "For what we are about to eat, we thank thee, Lord," he said.

"Amen," said all the family.

Mr. Meade's little prayer was over so

quickly that I didn't have time to feel uncomfortable about it. Ruthi and I never say any prayers before we eat our meals.

Edward and Timothy sat side by side. They are both big, far bigger than any young men I know in New York. Their faces are burned brown by the sun, and that makes their teeth look very white when they smile. I could see their arm muscles, developed from all their manual work on the farm.

"You mustn't fall in love with Eddie," Nell warned me. "He's courting Libby Greene, who lives down the road. But Tim is not sweet on anyone yet," she said.

The two brothers laughed at Nell's words. "It's a good thing I haven't made any announcements about what I think of the girls around here," Timothy said.

"Who do you like? Is it Hannah Sawyer? Or Martha Joy? Amy Bentley?" Nell began rattling off a long list of girls.

"You'll see that our Nell thinks out loud," said Mrs. Meade.

"She could get in big trouble doing that,"

said Emma disapprovingly. "Talk less and say more," she told her sister.

"Now, help yourself to everything," said Mrs. Meade, changing the subject and pointing to all the bowls and plates of food spread out on the table.

"Mother is an excellent cook," said Mr. Meade proudly, referring to his wife.

"Let me give you some meat," said Mrs. Meade, putting a large slice of something on my plate.

"What is it?" I asked suspiciously as I looked at the piece of meat that was taking up so much room on my dish. Ruthi said that I should feel free to eat anything at the Meades' home. By that I knew she meant I didn't have to worry about whether or not the food was kosher. Ruthi and I don't do very much to observe the fact that we are Jews. We can't observe the Sabbath because if she didn't work on Saturdays, she'd lose her job. But out of respect for Papa and Mama's memory, I've said that I'll never eat any meat from a pig.

"It's smoked ham," said Mrs. Meade. "Father

slaughtered the pig and smoked the meat himself."

Luckily they all were busy serving themselves and eating, so I don't think they noticed my shudder.

"You won't find a sweeter piece of ham anywhere in the state," Mrs. Meade said proudly.

"I'm not very hungry," I lied. I reached for the bread that was resting near me on the table. I knew bread would be safe for me to eat.

"Do you like applesauce? Coleslaw? Pickles?" Mrs. Meade kept pushing bowls toward me.

I ate a bit of everything but did not touch the ham. I glanced up and noticed Timothy looking over at my plate. I was keeping my food from touching the dreaded ham slice, which took up so much room. Suddenly he reached across the table and with his fork lifted the meat and put it on his own plate. I looked at him in amazement, and he winked at me.

"Have another slice of meat," said Mr. Meade when he noticed the ham had disappeared from my plate.

"Oh, no, no, no," I protested.

"I would hate eating our pigs," said Nell. "They always start out as such darling babies. So when it's time to slaughter them, we trade with our neighbors. This one wasn't ours. It was the Turners' pig."

"They all taste the same," Emma pointed out.

I knew I owed the Meades an explanation for not eating their food. Otherwise I would have to worry about every meal I ate in their home. I cleared my throat and wondered how best to make my excuses. "I'm sorry," I said. "But I just can't eat your ham. It's against my religion," I explained shyly.

"Really?" asked Mrs. Meade, surprised. "I never heard of such a thing."

"Maybe you don't know that I'm Jewish," I told her.

"Well, I suspected as much from your name," said Mrs. Meade as she helped herself to some more applesauce. "But we don't mind that. The world is big enough for all kinds of people," she added.

"Well, Jewish people don't ever eat pork," I

said, looking over at Mr. Meade, who was busy chewing a mouthful of food. He was the one who had prepared this meat for his family. "I'm sure it's very good. But I just can't eat it." Then I thought of something else I'd better tell the Meades. "When Jewish people eat meat, we don't have milk at the same meal. That's because it says we shouldn't in the Bible."

"Mary Wells ate ham. I saw her at the church supper," said Nell.

"Just because Mary Wells and Hadassah both come from New York City doesn't mean that they're the same," said Emma. "We never saw a Jewish person before. There aren't any around here."

"Not in Jericho," said Mrs. Meade. "But I know there are some Jewish families in Burlington. I even went into a shop owned by a Jewish man one time. He spoke with me and seemed very pleasant. I bought our sleigh blanket at his shop."

I smiled at Mrs. Meade. Then I looked over at Emma. She was looking at me suspiciously, as if I had suddenly taken on a new appearance since we had first met when I got off the train.

"Does that mean you're not a Christian?" she asked me.

I nodded my head.

"We read about the Jewish people in Sunday school," said Timothy. "The Old Testament is filled with stories about them: Sometimes they're called Israelites, and sometimes they're called Hebrews. You remember reading about Moses and Solomon and King David?" he said to his sisters. "They were all Jewish, just like Hadassah."

"Are you a princess?" Nell asked excitedly.

"A princess?"

"Well, if you're related to King David, you must be a princess."

Everyone laughed at Nell.

"No, I'm not a princess. I'm just a plain girl from the Lower East Side of New York." I didn't add that we were so poor that almost all my clothing was castoffs from other people, that my sister worked six days a week to support us, that we lived in a single room in someone else's apartment, that the food on the table before me now was more than Ruthi and I consumed in a week.

"Thank goodness you're not a princess," said Mrs. Meade. "I wouldn't know how to treat you if you were, and we'd have to spend all our time making curtsies and kissing your hand."

"Well, please don't worry or fuss about what I eat either. I'm sure there will always be something on the table that I can take for my meal." I smiled at Mrs. Meade. She was not at all like Mama, yet there was something about her that reminded me of my mother. Mama could always say something to bring a smile to my lips. I guessed that if I had to go away from home for two weeks, I was lucky to have been sent to this woman's house.

We heard a rumble of thunder in the distance.

"Better check that the windows are closed," said Mrs. Meade. "It sounds as if we're going to have some rain."

"I knew it!" shouted Nell with delight. "I told you that when the cows are lying down, it means it will rain."

"There are smart cows in Vermont," I said, nodding my head. I looked across at Emma. She is close to me in age and should be a friend, but she was busy stacking plates to take from the table and didn't look my way when I spoke. I don't know if she is shy or if she doesn't like me.

It seems as if the Meade family is divided into two sorts of people: talkers and nontalkers. Mrs. Meade and Nell and Timothy are the talkers. Mr. Meade and Eddie and Emma are the quiet ones. It's hard to know what they're thinking. I don't care too much about Mr. Meade and Eddie, but I wish Emma would talk to me more. I have a feeling she doesn't like me.

I think I'll read some of the messages in my autograph album. They will remind me of the people who do care about me back home.

At least I've made it through the first evening. Only thirteen more days until I'll be back on the train and going home to Essex Street again.

From My Autograph Album

Best wishes to one of my brightest students for a very bright future ahead.

Your teacher, Cynthia Blythe

∽∾∽∾∽∾∽∾∽∾∽∾∽∾∽∾∽∾∽∾∽∾∽∾∽∾∽∾∽∾

It only takes a little spot to write the words, Forget-me-not.

Your friend, Mimi Sosnov

∽∾∽∾∽∾∽∾∽∾∽∾∽∾∽∾∽∾∽∾∽∾∽∾∽∾∽∾∽∾

I wish you every possible happiness.

Your loving sister, Ruthi

∽∾∽∾∽∾∽∾∽∾∽∾∽∾∽∾∽∾∽∾∽∾∽∾∽∾∽∾∽∾

A few lines just for you:

_____

_____

_____

Your classmate, Milton Kazinski

August 2, 1910

I'd been rocked to sleep for so many hours on the train that I was sure I would have trouble sleeping last night. Also, I was afraid I'd feel lonely in the dark. I have never before had a bed all to myself. Even if I sometimes complain about Ruthi's bossiness, and that she takes up too much room in our bed, still I'm accustomed to the warmth of her body next to mine. It's a great comfort if I wake in the middle of the night from a bad dream to have her so close.

They do not have gaslight here, as we do at

home, so Mrs. Meade gave me a kerosene lamp and showed me how to use it. The rain had stopped, and there was some natural light too. I unpacked my clothing. The ink hadn't spilled! And I took out my books. I had read the whole of *Anne of Green Gables* during the train ride. It is a fine story. Imagine, Anne is an orphan with red hair, just like me. Even more of a coincidence, she goes off to stay with strangers. If only my stay with the Meades could turn out to be as successful as Anne's time in Green Gables. I plan to read the book again on the way home.

The other book I borrowed from the library is *Little Women*. I've already read it three times during the past couple of years. Louisa May Alcott is my favorite author. I've read all her books that the library owns. It's good to have Jo and Meg and Beth and Amy in the room here with me. Of course, I have the family portrait and my autograph album as well. It means I'm not alone after all.

I took out this journal and wrote about all that had happened since I got off the train. Then, at last, I changed into my nightgown and lay down on the bed. Its softness surprised me, for it was like nothing I'd ever felt before. At home Ruthi and I sleep on a thin, worn, sour-smelling mattress. Here the blanket and mattress both smelled of flowers.

The next thing I knew, the sun was coming through the small attic window. I can't remember having ever wakened that way before. The cracked window in our room on Essex Street looks out onto the brick wall of the building next door. Ruthi doesn't clean the window for fear that it will break, so it gets dirtier and darker all the time. Even if the window was clean, we could never tell if the sun was shining or not. I looked out the attic window and saw the Meades' cows grazing in the distance.

I didn't see anyone. I listened and didn't hear the sound of other people either. I decided that I must have wakened very early. Only the cows and I were awake! So I took my autograph album and reread each of the pages. I'm so glad to have it with me. I wonder if I'll feel close enough to the Meade family to ask them to sign in my album when it's time for me to return home.

Now I think I hear voices in the distance. Could I have been wrong? Perhaps I didn't wake early. There are none of the sounds that I'm accustomed to at home to give me a clue. There are no shouts from the iceman or the vegetable seller. No loud cries of the Aronson baby in the next room. No squabbling shouts from the other children. They are always making a racket. Perhaps it's very late. I think I must close my ink bottle and go downstairs. But I confess I'm afraid. It will be rude if I'm early and it will be rude if I'm late. But what can I do? I can't spend my whole day writing here in this room. Besides, my stomach is rumbling. I feel hungry.

Same day, after supper

When I went downstairs, I discovered I was both early and late. It was late if I was a farm-hand and had to milk the cows. Both Eddie and Timothy had done their morning chores and were finished with breakfast. But Emma and Nell were still asleep.

Mrs. Meade was busy in the corner. She waved a floury hand at me and said, "I am kneading the dough for some bread. Help yourself to breakfast. Everything's on the table."

I looked and saw another feast. There were two kinds of bread. Why did she *need* more? There was also a large chunk of butter, a bowl of preserves, boiled eggs, cold sliced ham, cheese, and a pitcher of milk.

"Could I help you in some way?" I offered, even though I do not know how to make bread. Ruthi always buys ours at the bakery on Allen Street.

"It's hard to work with an empty stomach," said Mrs. Meade. "My boys are always complaining that they're expected to milk the cows before breakfast. The trouble is they don't want to get up early enough to eat before their morning chores begin." She thought for a moment. "There is one thing you could do. Would you please break this egg into the bowl and beat it up for me? I want to brush some egg on the finished loaves, and I forgot to prepare it."

"Of course," I said. I walked over to her work area and found the bowl and egg waiting. I cracked the egg on the side of the bowl and emptied the contents into the bowl. "Oh, heavens!" I gasped, dropping the shell.

"What's wrong?" asked Mrs. Meade, alarmed at my tone.

I pointed inside the bowl. There were two bright yellow yolks staring up at us. They looked like a pair of golden eyes! "I never saw such a thing," I said. "What happened? Can you still use the egg?"

Mrs. Meade looked into the bowl for a moment and then began to laugh. She threw her floury arms around my neck. "You poor silly child," she said, laughing. "Have you never seen a double-yolked egg before?"

I shook my head.

"Of course not," she said. "I forgot that a city child like you will not have seen a lot of things. If you're lucky you may even see a triple-yolker before you return home."

Flushed with embarrassment, I quickly beat the egg for Mrs. Meade. Then I sat down at the table and put a thick slice of bread on my plate. I spread it with butter and added a bit of strawberry preserves. When I took the first bite, I thought I had never tasted anything so delicious in my life.

"This is the best thing I've ever eaten," I said as soon as I swallowed what I was chewing. Then I worried that she would think I didn't appreciate the dinner she served me last night. But the truth was, I was less nervous eating by myself and not being watched by all the family. Besides, the bread was so fresh it just dissolved in my mouth. Ruthi always buys the leftover stale bread that the bakery sells for a cheaper price.

"Pour yourself a glass of milk," said Mrs. Meade. She was putting the dough into the baking pans.

I did not drink any milk last night, so I was in for a surprise. The milk is completely different from the watery liquid that we buy at home.

"It's from our own cows, of course," said Mrs. Meade. "Tim said he would let you try to milk one before you go home."

"Really?" I asked, horrified. I thought of the big animals I had seen out in the fields. I don't think I want to touch one of them.

I heard footsteps on the stairs. Emma and Nell had come for their breakfast too.

"Hadassah! Here you are!" Nell shouted when she saw me. "We were being so quiet when we got dressed because we didn't hear any sound from your room. I even listened at the door because Emma wouldn't let me knock and wake you."

"Please knock tomorrow," I said. I smiled at Emma, but she just stared at me and did not return my smile.

The rest of the day passed with a hundred new sights, sounds, smells, and tastes. After breakfast Emma had to wash the glass chimneys and the lantern globes of the kerosene lamps. Nell's daily job is to search for eggs. So she grabbed a basket and took me on a tour of the entire farm. Just outside the house is a protected area filled with the most enormous pile of wood. "What is this for?" I asked. "Is your father going to build something?"

"That's the wood we'll burn in the winter," said Nell.

"You mean you'll burn all that wood?" I asked.

"Oh, yes," Nell informed me. "It was cut a year ago and seasoned. My father and brothers have to start cutting and splitting the wood for next year. Without it we'd freeze in the cold weather. Mama needs the wood for cooking too. Sometimes she calls it gopher wood."

"Gopher? Isn't that a kind of animal?" I asked.

"Gopher wood means we put one armful of wood into the stove and then we need to 'go for' another. It's Emma's and my job to keep the woodbox inside the house full."

"We burn coal in New York," I told her.

"What does coal look like?" Nell wanted to know. So I explained that it was like black rocks. She bent down and picked up a dark stone from the ground. "Like this?" she asked. I told her that coal was made out of some organic matter that had hardened over thousands of years. Luckily we had studied about it at school, so I could explain it a bit.

"It sounds funny," said Nell. I didn't tell her that some of the things I was learning about Vermont sounded funny to me.

We passed a small wooden house that Nell said was the icehouse. When she opened the door for me to take a look, a draft of cool air came out. Inside were huge blocks of ice, which Nell told me her father and brothers had cut in the winter from the pond behind the mill. I could see some shelves where Mrs. Meade stored the milk and meat to keep them cold.

"Archie, the iceman, drives his cart down our street every morning and sells ice to us," I told Nell. "When it's a hot day and he's in a good mood, he gives the little kids slivers of ice to suck on." I smiled, remembering Archie lifting the huge blocks of ice with his metal tongs.

Next we walked to a still-smaller wooden house, which was the chicken coop. Nell showed me how to look for eggs. We found an even dozen and put them inside the basket. One of them was cracked.

"That one is no good," Nell said when I handed it to her. "Mama will put it in the pig's mash."

"Why isn't it good?" I asked her. Ruthi always sends me to buy cracked eggs at the store.

"Dirt can get inside the crack," said Nell. "It could make you sick. Don't you know that?"

No, I didn't. And I decided I won't tell it to Ruthi either. Uncracked eggs cost twice as much as the cracked ones!

We stopped to look at the chickens. They were busy pecking at the ground and did not pay any attention to us at all. The pig, on the other hand, came up to the fence of his pen and stuck his snout through the wooden slats so that Nell could scratch him. "Now you can see why I would never want to eat him when he's full-grown," said Nell. "He's so sweet."

I would never think to describe the Meade pig as "sweet."

We looked in the barns, where I saw two cats but not Dandy, the horse, or any of the cows. "They're out in the pasture," Nell told me when I asked about them.

"Does your family own all this land?" I asked, awed by all I saw around me.

"We don't really have a big farm at all," Nell said. "We only have fifty-two acres. That's very small."

I've studied about acres at school, but I couldn't figure out the arithmetic in my head. All I know is that as far as I could see, the land belonged to the Meade family.

When we returned to the house, Mrs. Meade told Emma and Nell to weed the vegetable garden.

"Can I help too?" I asked.

"You'll be about as handy as a one-legged man in a kicking contest," Emma observed.

Mrs. Meade spoke up at once. "Emma, show Hadassah what the weeds look like," she said. "We don't want her to pull up all the carrot and tomato plants just because she's a city girl who doesn't know a weed from a window."

Once again my face flushed, and I felt awkward. It wasn't my fault that I didn't know what weeds look like.

"Do you want me to pick anything?" asked Emma.

"I want some carrots and beans for supper," said her mother. "Oh, and see if there's any rhubarb left. I'll make a pie for us if there is."

It was like magic. I watched as Emma pulled the orange carrots from the soil. She rubbed some of the dirt off with her hand before putting them in her basket. At school we learned about botany, but it is not the same as watching an actual edible plant pulled from the ground.

Emma pointed out the weeds. To tell the truth, they looked just like the green tops of the growing vegetables to me. "Could you eat weeds?" I asked.

"Of course not. They'd taste dreadful, and they'd make you sick," said Emma as if I were an idiot for even asking such a question. But I had a feeling she might be wrong about the weeds. After all, I eat cracked eggs and do not come to any harm.

"What's that?" I asked as she pulled up some reddish green stalks that resembled celery.

"Rhubarb," she responded.

"I've never seen that before," I said.

Emma broke a piece off and cleaned it on her skirt. "Taste it," she said.

I took a bite of the strange vegetable and chewed it down. At once my eyes began to tear from the sour taste and I felt myself gagging. I could not possibly bring myself to swallow it, and I spit the rhubarb out into my hand. How could the Meade family eat such an awful plant?

Nell laughed aloud. "Oh, Emma, that was mean," she said, but she seemed delighted by the trick her sister had played on me. "No one eats raw rhubarb. We cook it with lots of sugar, and then it tastes wonderful."

I threw the half-chewed rhubarb I was holding onto the ground and wiped my hand on the handkerchief that was in my skirt pocket.

"Why are you so nasty to me?" I asked Emma. I kept my eyes down on my handkerchief so she couldn't see the tears that had come into my eyes.

Emma backed away from me. When I finally looked at her, I saw that for once it was her face that had turned red. "Sorry," she mumbled. "It was just a little joke. I thought it would be funny."

"You better be careful," Nell warned her sister. "Hadassah will probably think of a joke of her own to get back at you."

"I don't want to get back at you," I said to both sisters. "I'm not like that. I can't help it if I'm ignorant about your plants. I bet there are lots of things I know about city life that you never heard of."

Emma shrugged her shoulders, but Nell said, "You could tell us about them. Maybe someday we'll visit a big city. So far I haven't even been to Burlington, but Mama says we'll go there one of these days. All right, Hadassah?" She took my hand and squeezed it.

I was still feeling annoyed with Emma, but I couldn't help liking Nell. She was so sweet. It would be fun to have a younger sister like her, I thought. "Why don't you call me Dossi?" I said to the sisters. "That's what everyone calls me at home."

"Dossi, Dossi," said Nell, trying it out. "I like that. It sounds friendlier than Hadassah."

I looked at Emma.

"But we're not friends yet," she said to her sister.

Now, as I sit here writing, I keep thinking about Emma's manner. It is almost as if there were one of those Vermont stone walls separating us. I wonder if it will come down before it's time for me to return home. I wonder if we'll ever be friends.

August 3, 1910

*L*ast night it was so hot that I couldn't sleep. The bed that had seemed so comfortable the night before was now damp with my sweat. My nightdress stuck to me, and a mosquito kept buzzing by my head. At home we have a thousand roaches. I hate them, but at least they have the good sense to be silent.

Finally, after tossing one way and another, I got up and walked toward the open window. I hoped there would be a little breeze to cool me. It was dark, but not so dark that I couldn't find my way.

I rested my arms on the window ledge and looked out. I wondered if I was facing in the direction of New York City and Ruthi. I had gotten through my first full Vermont day, but now that it was night, I missed Ruthi so much. Perhaps if I concentrated very hard, she could hear my thoughts. Perhaps she would write and tell me to come home to her. It was a silly thought, but that's what was in my head at that moment.

Suddenly a spark of light flashed past my eyes. Then it was gone. I thought I must have imagined it, but at once there was another spark. My heart began to beat with fear. Could there be a fire? I didn't smell any smoke, but still, I thought I should warn someone. It would be awful if the house burned down with all the family inside just because I hadn't said a word.

I made my way in the dark to the doorway and called out, "Emma, Nell." Then I called again, louder, "Emma. Nell. Wake up!"

A door opened, and a moment later a bit of light shone on the landing.

"What is it?" asked Emma. She was wearing

a long white nightgown and holding a kerosene lamp.

"There's a fire," I said anxiously. "Come. I'll show you."

I grabbed her by the arm and pulled her toward my window. "Look at those sparks," I said, pointing out into the darkness where more sparks than ever were now visible.

"Oh, Hadassah, you foolish girl," scolded Emma. "Those aren't sparks at all. They're fire-flies."

"Fireflies?" I asked, puzzled. "Do they bring fire?"

"Haven't you seen a firefly before?" she asked in amazement. Nell had joined us, and she began to laugh.

"You don't have to be afraid of them," Nell said. "They're just little bugs. And they're perfectly harmless. They don't even sting or bite like bees or mosquitoes."

I stared out the window at the bits of light.

"Come," Nell said. "We'll show you."

Silently I followed Emma and Nell down the stairs. Emma led the way with her lamp. Nell opened the door, and we walked outside.

The ground felt cool and damp on my bare feet. I stepped on something sharp and called out with the unexpected pain.

"Hush!" snapped Emma. "You don't want to wake the rest of the family, do you?"

Neither she nor Nell seemed to think it was strange for us to be walking outside with bare feet or in our nightgowns. But I thought it would be awful if Eddie and Timothy saw me this way.

"It's wet," I said softly as we walked into the long grass at the side of the house. I lifted my nightgown to keep it dry.

"Do," Emma said.

"Do? What do you want me to do?" I did not understand.

"Not *do*. It's *d-e-w*," Emma explained. "It's the moisture that forms on the grass at night."

Nell rushed ahead and called out, "Here! I caught one. Come and see."

Emma held the lamp close so I could look inside the cup of her sister's hands. There was a small insect. Even as I peered at it, a glow shone forth between Nell's fingers.

"It's magic," I said as Nell opened her hands and let the insect fly free again.

"No. Just a bug," said Emma. "Next time you'll know what it is you're seeing."

I looked up and saw the sky was dotted with a thousand sparks of light. But those were lights that I could recognize. "I never saw so many stars in all my life," I told the sisters.

"This must be very different from your home in the city," Nell commented.

I nodded in the dark.

We stood together in silence, admiring the points of light in the sky. Suddenly I sneezed.

"Oh, dear. You mustn't get a chill," said Nell. She hooked her arm in mine and steered me toward the house.

"Are you having a good time here?" she asked.

"Oh, yes," I said politely. And suddenly I realized that for the past half hour I had not once thought about Ruthi or Essex Street and I *had* been enjoying myself. It was nice of the Meade sisters to get out of bed in the night to show me those strange fireflies. In the dark

Emma seemed to be having a good time too. She hadn't complained that I had wakened her. Maybe I imagined that she didn't like me. Maybe I would have a good time here after all, I thought hopefully as I climbed into bed.

Just before I fell asleep, I wondered if my feet were dirty. I knew that Ruthi would not have been pleased if I soiled the fresh bed-clothes.

Now I am awake and dressed and waiting for Emma and Nell to knock on the door and tell me it's time to begin my next day here in Jericho.

Mount Lebanon Academy
P.O. Box 10357
Pittsburgh, PA 15234

Lake Champlain from "Red Rocks", Burlington, Vt.

August 4, 1910

Dear Mimi,

    You would be amazed at all the animals that are here—cows, chickens, horses, pigs, cats. Yesterday evening I saw a pair of wild deer run across the field and into the woods. Every day I seem to see or discover something new. I'm having fun, but it would be even more fun if you were here too.

    I wonder who you are spending your time with while I'm away. Do you miss me?

Your friend,
Dossi

August 4, 1910

*H*ere are some of the things that happened yesterday. At breakfast Nell said to me, "Why did you bring all your *old* clothes for your visit here? Mary Wells wore a new dress or skirt almost every time we saw her."

I looked down at the skirt I was wearing. It was the same one I had arrived in and worn the day before. I have only one other skirt with me. They're all I own except for a heavy woolen one that once belonged to Ruthi. I didn't bring that because we decided it would be too hot for this time of year.

"You can't judge a man by his overcoat," said Mrs. Meade to her younger daughter in a sharp voice.

I'm not a man, and I wasn't wearing an overcoat, but I knew what she meant. Still, I was mortified by Nell's words, and my eyes filled with tears.

Mrs. Meade continued speaking. "Mary Wells was foolish to bring so much good clothing with her. You told me yourself that she got mud on her skirts and even tore one of them the day you all went to pick blueberries."

I blinked away my tears and smiled my thanks at Mrs. Meade for defending me. She must have guessed about my wardrobe. Everyone knows that the Fresh Air Fund is a charity for poor city children. Mary Wells probably borrowed clothing from everyone she knew, the way Ruthi borrowed a shawl from Mrs. Aronson and a necklace from Mrs. Lefkowitz the evening Meyer Reisman took her to the free concert at Cooper Union last winter.

Later in the morning Emma, Nell, and I went walking together down the road to the post office and the general store on some errands for Mrs. Meade. I was pleased when Emma began to ask me questions.

"I'm getting used to the fact that you're not a Christian," she admitted to me. "It seemed so surprising at first. I guess we must seem strange to you too."

Her comment didn't really make me uncomfortable. It showed she had some interest in me. "You don't seem strange," I said. "You all seem very nice. I like your family very much."

"Are we the first Christians that you've met?" Emma asked.

"No," I replied. "In my school there are both Christian and non-Christian students. And all of my teachers are Christian."

"New York must be so different from our little town," Emma commented. "Tell us about New York City," she asked me shyly. "It's hard for us to imagine what it's like."

"I don't know where to begin," I admitted. "It's so unlike your world here. It even smells different. Here I can smell the cows and the earth and the flowers. At home the odors are less pleasant. We live so close together that we breathe in our neighbors' sweat and what they're cooking for their supper." I paused a moment. "But not all the smells are bad," I added, defending my home. "I love to walk along Delancey Street and sniff the barrels of sour pickles and the herrings that the vendors have lined up in front of their shops."

"I like pickles too," Nell said. "Mama makes them every year."

"Tell us more," Emma coaxed me.

"I often walk great distances," I told her. "Sometimes my friend Mimi comes with me. There is a huge park in the middle of the city. It has hundreds of trees and grass and flowers. There is even a lake. But it's several miles from where we live. If we take the tram, then we have no money for a cold drink. So we always have to decide which we care about more, our feet or our thirst."

I smiled at the girls as I remembered one of our walks. "One day we walked from our house all the way to Forty-second Street to see the grand new public library that is being built on the site of the reservoir there. That was a long walk too. More than three miles each way."

"We have a library here. It's housed in a room in Miss Peabody's home," Emma told me. "It's open two days a week for three hours each time."

That surprised me. I'm glad to know a way in which New York is superior to Jericho, Vermont. The library I go to is open six days a week and for many hours.

"I brought two books with me from the branch of the library near my home," I said. I told her the titles.

"I've already read *Little Women*," Emma said. "And I read some other books by Louisa May Alcott too. But I never heard of *Anne of Green Gables*."

"It's a very good story," I told her. "I was so involved reading it on the train that I didn't even realize where I was. I looked up expecting to be in my room at home and was amazed to see so many strangers walking about."

"That's funny," said Nell.

"That's happened to me when I read a good

book," Emma said. "I enter the world of the story I'm reading."

I thought of something. "Would you like to borrow *Anne of Green Gables* from me while I'm here?" I offered. "I'm sure you'll enjoy it too."

"Oh, yes," Emma said eagerly. I was delighted that I had found something that I could share with her.

We walked along quietly for a time. Nell stopped and picked wildflowers along the dirt road.

"What are you doing that for? We have those same flowers growing on our property," Emma told her sister. But Nell just ignored Emma's comment and kept on picking.

After a bit Emma looked at me and spoke again. "Perhaps someday I'll go to New York City. Maybe I'll come and visit you," she said shyly.

"Me too," said Nell at once. "I want to see New York too."

I looked at them, horrified. I'd made a point of not describing my home to them. They had no idea about where I lived. It's not a big house with many rooms like theirs. Ruthi and I live in a single room in the Aronsons' apartment. Our meals are mostly cold—bread and cheese and cold meats that we buy and eat on the few plates we have. Sometimes in the winter Mrs. Aronson lets Ruthi make a pot of soup on her stove. Sometimes she offers us part of the meal she has prepared. We always pay for our share. What would Emma and Nell think of our life after all the space and riches they're accustomed to here?

"Perhaps," I said, and Emma immediately sensed my reluctance.

"That's not very generous of you," she said, sounding annoyed.

"That's all right, Dossi. I like it here," said Nell. She shrugged.

But I could see I had offended Emma and I had lost my chance to become her friend.

I also noticed that while Nell had taken to calling me Dossi, Emma had not. It seemed a sign that she didn't want to become close to me.

Luckily someone on a bicycle rode past at the crossroad ahead of us, and it was a distraction. At first I thought it was a boy. But closer I could see his mustache and make out that it was a grown man. He lifted an arm and tipped his cap. "Good morning, ladies," he said as he went by.

Nell giggled. "He always calls us ladies," she whispered.

"Who is he?" I asked.

"Mr. Bentley," said Emma. "He's one of our neighbors. But everyone calls him Snowflake Bentley because he's so crazy about snow."

"He takes photographs of snowflakes. Isn't that strange?" asked Nell. "I bet you never heard of anyone doing that."

"That's true," I said. "I didn't know you could even do such a thing."

"We think he's a little bit touched in the head," said Nell. "You should take pictures of people. Not snowflakes!"

"Hush, Nell, that's not polite," Emma said, correcting her sister.

"You said so yourself," Nell protested. "I heard you talking about him with Tim one day."

"Never mind," said Emma.

"Mr. Bentley lives with his brother and his brother's family. And all the children have names that begin with the letter *A*," Nell informed me. "There's Alric, Agnes, Arthur, Alice, Archie, Amy, Anna, and Alwyn. Isn't that amazing?"

I agreed. "It's funny, but you know that there're three children in your family with names starting with *E*—Edward, Emma, and Nell's real name is Eleanor. Suppose your parents had given Timothy an *E* name too?"

So all the rest of the way to the post office, we suggested names to one another that Mr. and Mrs. Meade could have given their younger son—Edgar, Edwin, Emmett, Edmund, Elliott, Elmer. . . .

But the coolness and angry words that Emma had said to me were still there between us. I can't forget them, and I'm certain neither can she.

From My Autograph Album

Be not false, unkind, or cruel.
Banish evil words or strife.
Thus shall each day be a jewel
Strung upon the thread of life.
                    Your friend, Nellie Kenyon

Remember me in friendship
Remember me in love
Remember me dear Dossi
When we meet in Heaven above.
                    Your seatmate, Helen Miller

May your voyage through life
Be as happy and free
As the dancing waves
On the deep blue sea.
                    Your schoolmate, Edith Thorn

When you glance at this page
Don't get angry and frown
For 'tis written by one
Who wrote upside down.
                    Your classmate, Nicholas Snyder

August 5, 1910

*W*henever I feel a bit lonely or unhappy, I turn to the pages of my autograph album. Then I can imagine the faces of my schoolmates, and it makes me smile.

Unfortunately today this remedy doesn't seem to work. That's because, in addition to being unhappy, I'm feeling unwell. During the night, I had to run downstairs twice to use the privy. There's a chamber pot here in my room, but I couldn't bring myself to use it. This morning too I've had to rush to the privy again.

Mrs. Meade diagnosed my ailment at once. "Our food is too rich for your poor stomach," she said. "I should have thought to dilute the milk you drink with water. It's a wonder you didn't get sick the very first night."

I thought back and realized that I haven't drunk milk with every meal the way Emma and Nell do. When there is meat on the table, I avoid the milk pitcher. That prevented me from being ill sooner.

So here I am, lying in my bed. Emma brought me a plate with a slice of unbuttered bread and a cup of hot tea. I thanked her, but I have no appetite to eat anything. I did take a few sips of the tea, however.

"Could I borrow that book you brought?" she asked me. I nodded.

"I hope you like it," I said as she took the book from the top of the dresser, where I had left it.

Then Nell came into the room with a few pretty wildflowers in a glass. She put them on the chest and whispered to me, "It's boring without you."

I reached out my arms and gave her a hug.

"You don't have to whisper," I told her. "I'm not dying."

However, a little later I had to run downstairs to the privy once more. I did feel as if I were dying for a few moments. But the relief is great afterward. And just now I don't feel so bad at all.

I hope I'm recovered by this evening. Nell came upstairs a second time to tell me that we have all been invited to go to the Bentleys' house after dinner. "He plays the piano, and we all sing," she informed me.

"Who plays the piano?" I asked.

"Mr. Bentley." Then she giggled and added, "Snowflake. He's the one you saw on the road yesterday."

Same day, late evening

I'm so thankful that my stomach was no longer bothering me this evening. At suppertime I was cautious and ate only a little bread and cheese and drank a cup of tea. As soon as the dishes were cleared from the table, all of us walked up the road to the Bentley house.

It's a large farmhouse, not unlike the Meade home. I met all the Bentleys, including the many children with the initial A. The father of all these people is Mr. Charles Bentley, who is the brother of the man I saw riding the bicycle. Wilson Bentley, or Uncle Willie, as everyone calls him, is Mr. Charles Bentley's younger brother. The younger Mr. Bentley is quite short. In fact, I believe he is smaller than I am, despite the fact that I'm still growing and he's a grown man. From the back one would mistake him for a boy. Then, when he turns around, you're surprised to see his big mustache.

It was the short Willie Bentley who made the gathering so much fun. He plays the piano. Nell says he often invites the Meades over for a musical evening. Everyone sat about, singing merry tunes. It was delightful to see Eddie and Timothy joining in with the singing. Even silent Mr. Meade sang out with a fine deep voice.

Mr. Bentley played "Meet Me in St. Louis," "Daisy, Daisy," "Yankee Doodle," and many other songs that I learned at school, so I was able to take part in the singing too. I enjoyed myself very much.

After the music Mrs. Charles Bentley served lemonade and slices of pound cake. They looked delicious, but just in time I remembered my stomach problems and refrained from eating anything.

"Don't you like cake?" inquired Uncle Willie when he saw me passing up the refreshments.

"I love cake. But I'm not hungry this evening," I told him. I didn't wish to seem impolite, but of course I couldn't discuss my upset stomach with him.

"I hope you're enjoying your stay in Vermont," he said.

"It's a very beautiful place," I told him, "and the Meade family is very kind to take me in."

"We try to have one or two young people come and stay at our farm each year too," he said. "The Fresh Air Fund is a wonderful organization. If I were a millionaire, I would surely endow it."

"Emma told me that you've photographed snowflakes," I said. "I didn't know one could do such a thing."

"No one knew. Or at least no one bothered to try," Mr. Bentley replied. "But I've been doing it since I was a young man with my first camera. And do you know what I have discovered? No two snowflakes are ever alike."

"Really?" I thought back to the falling snow in New York City last winter and marveled at what he said. All that snow certainly appeared the same to me.

"Come over sometime during the day," he suggested. "I'll show you some of the pictures I've taken to prove what I've just said. You'll be amazed at the beauty and delicacy of the flakes."

"Oh, thank you," I said, delighted by his offer. "I would love to see them before I return to New York."

It was getting late, so we departed soon afterward. Mr. Meade carried a kerosene lantern to light our way, as it was now very dark.

"Hey, Red," Timothy called out to me. He's been teasing me because of my red hair. "Let me teach you a trick for walking in the dark. Put your whole foot down, instead of the usual way of walking, which is to place your heel on the ground, followed by your toe. That way your toe won't trip over a rock or fallen branch that you can't see."

I walked carefully, using Timothy's method. It must have worked, because I didn't stumble a single time in the dark. All around us were tiny sparks of light. Now I knew what they were and I could delight in their mysterious lighting. No kerosene lamps for them!

I hope I'll have an opportunity to see Mr. Bentley's photographs before I go back home.

August 6, 1910

$\mathscr{S}$omething quite awful happened today. It was an especially hot day, and after lunch Mrs. Meade suggested that Emma, Nell, and I go to the pond. Reluctantly I put on my swimming costume underneath my clothing. Emma and Nell did the same. Emma carried an old quilt for us to lie on in the sun.

"I'm taking your book," Emma informed me. "I'm halfway through. It's a very good story."

I was pleased she was enjoying the book. But at the same time I realized that, by taking it to read, she wouldn't have to talk to me. And I never guessed that, before the day was out, I would regret I'd ever let her borrow it.

As we walked, Nell and Emma taught me the names of the various wildflowers we passed. They're much more beautiful than the flowers planted in formal rows in Central Park. I learned to recognize Queen Anne's lace, black-eyed Susans, buttercups, devil's paintbrush, and goldenrod.

Even though I had protested to Ruthi about the swimming costume, I found that, once I was at the pond and standing next to Emma and Nell wearing matching bloomers, with their legs exposed like mine, I was not as self-conscious as I'd been when I tried the costume on at home. We all looked equally foolish. The pond water was deliciously cold. Nell splashed me, and I splashed her back. Before I knew it, I was as wet as if I'd taken a bath in the tub in Mrs. Aronson's kitchen.

While Nell and I continued playing in the water, Emma got out of the pond and sat down on the quilt to dry off in the sun. Nell and I splashed for several more minutes before we left the water. Emma was engrossed in my library book, but Nell and I danced about, shaking water off ourselves like a pair of dogs caught in the rain.

I heard a faint rumble of thunder, but when I asked if we should return to the house, both Emma and Nell assured me that it was far away. "Sometimes it will rain in Essex Center or in Underhill and we won't get even a single drop of water here," said Emma, looking up for a moment from the book.

I lay down on the blanket and felt the warm sun on my skin.

"Do you know any tongue twisters?" Nell asked me. She taught me a few that she knew.

A box of mixed biscuits, a mixed biscuit box.

Two toads totally tired tried to trot to Tedbury.

A swan swam over the sea; swan, swim; swan swam back again; well swum, swan.

It's a shame, Sam; these are the same, Sam. 'Tis all a sham, Sam, and a shame it is to sham so, Sam.

We repeated them many times and laughed at the way our tongues missed the words. After a bit, however, I became aware of a breeze cooling me. A dark cloud was approaching in the sky.

I shivered in my damp clothing, and I was sure it would rain on us soon, but certainly Emma and Nell knew more about their weather than I did. So I held my tongue. Suddenly there was a crack of thunder that was much, much closer than before.

"Oh, dear," shouted Emma, jumping up. "Help me with the quilt," she yelled to her sister. They quickly folded it, and we all grabbed our clothing. It began to rain as we ran back to the farmhouse, shouting and laughing, still dressed in our bathing costumes. We were totally soaked! Even our regular garments, which we held in our arms, were drenched by the rain. I had pinned my hair up before I went into the pond, but it had fallen down when I was running, and it was dripping down my back by the time we reached the house.

We rushed indoors, laughing and glad to be protected. As we dried ourselves, Mrs. Meade heated milk with honey in it for us to drink.

"You didn't need the pond to cool you off after all," she said to us. "And now that you're here, you can help me. I've begun canning our beans. You can trim the ends off them."

It was something I'd never seen before. We washed the freshly picked green beans. There were pounds and pounds of them. Then we cut the ends off, and Mrs. Meade dropped the beans into a pot of boiling water. She had another enormous pot on the stove with more boiling water. Into that she put the empty glass jars into which she later poured the beans. Then she fastened glass lids with metal wires that were attached to the jars. The jars were again placed in water and boiled to prevent spoilage.

The large kitchen became hot and steamy. It was tedious work, yet it was cozy to be working with the Meade women while the rain continued to pour down heavily outside. I wondered what Mr. Meade and Eddie and Timothy did in the rain. I didn't think they could work in the fields.

Afterward Mrs. Meade told Nell to show me the cupboards in the cellar where she stored her canned food. I was astounded. There were jars and jars of beans, corn, pickles, tomatoes, and spiced apples and strawberry preserves. The colors—green, yellow, and two shades of red—were revealed by the kerosene lamp in Nell's hand.

"This is what we eat all winter long," Nell said. "Every year we put up enough food to last for two years. That's in case one summer the crops fail and we can't put up anything."

"That's incredible," I said. "It's worth all the labor it takes." Then I noticed a row of tins. "What's inside those?" I asked.

"Maple syrup," Nell told me.

"I've read about it in a book. But I've never tasted any," I said.

"Never? What do you put on your pancakes in New York?" Nell wanted to know.

"I don't have pancakes," I said.

"Oh, how terrible," said Nell. "I'll tell Mama to make some before you go home. Everyone here loves them. You will too. I'm sure your religion won't mind your eating pancakes."

She led the way up the stairs, and I followed behind.

Emma and her mother were finished

putting the canning pots away. The jars of green beans were lined up on the worktable to cool. Mrs. Meade went off to her bedroom to change out of her sweat-soaked shirtwaist.

"Now I'm going to read until supper," said Emma. Suddenly a stricken look came across her face.

"What is it?" I asked her.

"I don't have the book," she said. "I left it by the pond."

"By the pond?" I asked, not believing what she had just said.

"Yes," said Emma quietly.

I felt sick. I had never seen a book that was left outside in a rainstorm, but I could imagine what it would look like. "How could you do that?" I whispered in horror. "You know it's not my book. I have to return it to the library as soon as I get home."

"I'll get it later when it stops raining," Emma promised.

"But it will look terrible," I cried out, my voice getting louder. "What am I going to do?"

"I don't know," said Emma. She grabbed my arm. "But if you're my friend, you won't dare tell my mother about this. And don't you be a tattletale either," she warned her sister.

"You don't care if I get into trouble, do you?" I said, full of anger. "You're awful!"

"You don't think *I'm* awful, do you?" asked Nell, pulling on my sleeve.

I shook my head, but I couldn't speak. I know that the librarian will never forgive me for mistreating her book. I have to buy a new copy. But where in the world will I ever get so much money?

August 7, 1910

*I*t's Sunday morning, and all the Meades are at church. I was invited to join them. Mrs. Meade was very kind. She immediately added that she would understand if I wished to remain at home. I confess that I'm a little curious about their church, but still, I felt it was not proper for me to spend the morning pretending to recite their Christian prayers. I'd also worry that I'd do something wrong.

So I watched the whole family depart, pulled by Dandy, in their wagon. They all were dressed in their best clothes. Eddie and Timothy had their hair slicked back with water and looked even more handsome wearing white shirts and jackets. Timothy winked at me as they left. "We'll miss you, Red," he said. As usual, my face flushed at his words. One of the problems of being a redhead is that I blush very easily.

Now I'm alone here (except for all the animals, of course). I've been thinking and thinking about the ruined library book. When Emma retrieved it yesterday evening from the ground near the pond, the pages were heavy with moisture and the cover was stained and swollen. "It will dry out," said Emma. Perhaps she's right, but it will never look the same. I know the librarian will be very annoyed with me when she sees the book. And I will have to replace it.

If Mrs. Meade had seen the book when Emma gave it to me, she would certainly have scolded her daughter. She probably would have made her pay for the new copy. But Emma was careful to give me the book when her mother wasn't about. And even though I'm furious at Emma, I can't bring myself to tell on her. I don't want to be a snitcher. Years ago at school we were taught not to tell on one another, and we learned the rhyme:

Tattletale tit
Your dog shall be split
And all the dogs in the town
Will have a little bit.

If only there was some way that I could confide in Mrs. Meade without letting her know that it was Emma's fault that the book was ruined. Perhaps she could think of a way to help me. Mrs. Meade has been so kind about everything and has been particularly concerned about my meals. She worries because I won't touch the ham or pork chops or sausage that are a regular part of the Meade diet. I told her that I am very happy to eat the wonderful fresh vegetables and the homemade bread and butter that are on the table at every meal. But that doesn't satisfy her. She makes every effort to prepare dishes that I'll be able to eat.

Last night she served a huge pot of chicken fricassee. It was one of their own chickens, which Mr. Meade had slaughtered in the morning. There was a thick rich sauce and carrots, green beans, and potatoes, all from their own garden. It's amazing to be as self-sufficient as the Meades are.

A few days ago Mrs. Meade made a pie with the rhubarb that Emma had picked in the garden.

"It's delicious," Nell assured me. "You won't believe it's the same sour plant that you bit into before."

"A small slice," I said to Mrs. Meade, who was cutting the pie into serving pieces.

Hesitantly I put the first forkful in my mouth. It was indeed delicious. Both sour and sweet at the same time. But as I was chewing the pie, Mrs. Meade suddenly said, "Hadassah. I just realized that I used lard to make the piecrust. Can you eat that?"

"What's lard?" I asked as I swallowed the pie in my mouth.

"Pig's fat," said Eddie.

I put the fork down on my plate. I couldn't eat another bite of that pie. But a moment later Timothy reached over and scooped the slice right off my plate. "I wish you'd asked for a bigger piece," he said, smiling at me.

"I'm so sorry," apologized Mrs. Meade. "It never occurred to me. I always use lard when I make piecrusts. But don't worry. I can use butter just as well."

I didn't remind her that Jewish people don't eat butter or dairy products at the same meal with meat. It was a problem I'd never had at home, because we have so little to eat that if there's butter, there's no meat. And if there's meat, there's no butter.

"Poor Dossi," said Nell sympathetically as she scraped the last crumbs of the pie from her plate.

"You don't have to worry about me," I reassured her and all the family. "I am eating so much that soon my skirt won't want to button on me in the morning."

"Good," said Mrs. Meade. "I don't want you

to return to New York looking as scrawny as when you arrived."

"Mama," Nell said, "that's not polite."

"Never mind," said her mother. "It's true."

Mount Lebanon Academy
P.O. Box 10357
Pittsburgh, PA 15234

August 3, 1910

Dearest Sister,

I trust this letter finds you well. I miss you very much, but it pleases me to think of you in the fresh air of Vermont.

Here on Essex Street all continues as usual. The weather has been very hot since you left, so I'm happy to think that you do not have to suffer from the heat. Yesterday Mrs. Aronson told me she is expecting another child in January. This will bring the total number of little Aronsons up to five. She said that I needn't worry and that we can continue to rent our room because, after all, a baby doesn't take up much space. But remembering all the crying and commotion that went on when little Shlomo was born, I have some good news that I hope will make you as happy as it makes me.

Meyer Reisman has asked me to marry him! You may think it's funny that he asked me just after you went away. The truth is I hoped very much that someday he would speak those words. I dreamed about it, yet I didn't tell you in case he didn't care for me as much as I have come to care for him. But when he saw me at a moment when I was especially lonely for you, he suddenly said if we married, I'd never be so alone again. He admits now that he worried that I did not feel as strongly as he did. Weren't we both foolish? Now I am very happy and hope my news will please you as well. Soon we'll once again be part of a real family, and it will not be just the two of us alone.

Do you remember when I first met Meyer over a year and a half ago? It was when I went to buy some syrup to relieve that bad cough you had. He spoke with me that evening, and a friendship began that has grown and grown since then. I have learned a great deal about him, and that is how I have come to be so fond of him.

Although he is only twenty-eight, Meyer is a widower. His wife died in labor during a difficult childbirth four years ago. The infant died too. He was very unhappy and for a long time didn't think he would ever remarry. Then he met me! Because of the tragedy in his life, he has a compassion for and an understanding of our losses. He understands that to marry me means that he gains not only a wife but a sister too. And that the sister will live with us. He insisted on that even before I told him that this would be a condition to my marriage. We both know that were it not for you and your sore throat, we might never have met—though I admit it seems strange to think of any illness with gratitude.

So it's to Meyer's three-room apartment on First Avenue that we'll move after I marry him next winter. It's strange, but I feel as if I've known him all my life. I love him and know that you will too. Remember that beautiful Sunday in March when it was my birthday? Meyer arrived carrying a bouquet of flowers and the strudel cake, which the three of us ate together. You could see then that he has both a warm manner and a hearty laugh.

In fact, I must now confess that it was Meyer who first told me about the Fresh Air Fund holidays. He suggested that I consider the benefits for you of a summer in a wholesome environment. He said that he himself went on such holidays over several summers when he was your age. He stayed with a family in a rural community in upstate New York. (The father was a pharmacist, and it was he who encouraged Meyer to study in this area.) So now you see that your new brother-to-be has already had an influence on your life, and it is due to his urging that you are enjoying your current stay in Vermont.

Meyer says that after we marry, he wants me to give up my job at the shirt factory. "What about the money I earn?" I said. "I want Dossi to continue her education. Perhaps even to go to college."

"My new sister will have money for college," he promised me. To prove it, this evening he showed me a bankbook for an account that he has just opened in your name at the Bank of the Manhattan Company. He has deposited fifty dollars in it and promises to add more every year. That certainly proves that your brother-to-be is also generous.

I've never written such a long letter in my life. I could go on and on for many more pages telling you about Meyer. However, you'll be getting to know him very well soon enough. We'll both be at the train station to meet you when you return. In the meantime he joins me in saying he hopes you are having a fine visit. We will see you soon.

Your affectionate sister,
Ruthi

August 9, 1910

So much has happened since I last wrote. Last night I had trouble falling asleep. I couldn't lie still on the soft mattress. I turned and turned, thinking about so many things. First of all there was the letter that had come that day from Ruthi. Emma and Nell and I had walked to the post office to get Mr. Meade's weekly paper and whatever else the post might bring. Mrs. Meade was hoping for a letter from her sister, who lives in Springfield, Massachusetts. Instead there was a letter for me from *my* sister.

Nell wanted me to open it at once. "I've

never received a letter," she said enviously.

"Neither have I," I admitted. Though I was very eager to read Ruthi's message, I wanted to read it in the privacy of my bedroom and not share it with anyone. So I put it in my pocket and waited impatiently till after lunch.

When I read Ruthi's words, I felt dizzy. Our whole life is about to change because my sister is going to get married! Who is this Meyer Reisman that he can upset our life so drastically? Of course I've met him a couple of times. But I don't really *know* him at all, only his outward appearance. He's short and beginning to lose his hair. I think when I get married, I'll want my husband to be more handsome. Perhaps he'll look something like Timothy Meade, tall and tanned and with a thick head of hair. I can't imagine living with Meyer Reisman, and now I must share my sister with him.

And how dare he demand that Ruthi give up her job at the factory? I can remember how delighted she was when she was hired there.

Ruthi says that Meyer is kind and generous and that I will grow to love him too. I wonder if this is so. Do I need a brother? And isn't Ruthi too young to get married? It's true that our parents were married when Mama was just seventeen, a full year younger than Ruthi. Still, that was in Russia. Life was different there. The unexpectedness of Ruthi's news churns in my stomach just as the rich food did a few days ago. It will take some time until I can adjust to it all.

There's something else in Ruthi's letter for me to think about. She writes about my going to college. In June Miss Blythe told me that I must seriously consider continuing my education. She said I was too good a student to drop out of school the moment the law said I was old enough to do so. That got me thinking, and I told Ruthi that I would like to be a teacher instead of a factory worker. Now I know that she has never forgotten those words of mine.

As if all this weren't enough, I had a more immediate problem to worry about as well— my library book. The pages are drying out. But it is no longer the perfect new book that I borrowed from the library.

"Oh, Hadassah, I'm so sorry," Emma said

when we looked at it together yesterday. "You know I didn't do it on purpose."

"Of course I know that," I said sourly, "but that won't make a difference when I take the book into the library." As far as I'm concerned, every page of that book shows Emma's carelessness. I worry that I'll never be permitted to borrow another volume from the library. What an awful punishment that would be!

While I tossed in bed, troubled by all these different thoughts, it grew later and later. Suddenly I became aware of a smoky odor in the air. Was Mr. Meade standing in front of the house and smoking his pipe? I wondered.

I got out of bed and went to my window. The night was dark without a moon, and I couldn't see anyone below. I listened for footsteps. There was nothing. Then off in the distance I saw a flash of light. It must be one of those fireflies, I thought. Then I saw it again. It was not the golden light of the insect but a red glow. There was a real fire somewhere nearby.

Although the night was warm, I shivered with fear. I rushed to the door across the hall and knocked loudly. "Emma. Nell," I shouted.

Then I turned the knob and opened it. "There's a fire!" I called to the sleeping sisters inside the room. "Help me wake everyone."

I heard a match strike, and a moment later Emma had lit the kerosene lamp beside the bed.

"Hadassah Rabinowitz," she said harshly, "is that all you can do? Imagine fires every night?"

"No, no. This isn't like last time. This is a real fire. I'm certain of it."

"I smell smoke," said a sleepy voice. It was Nell.

Emma took a deep breath. "I think you're right," she conceded. "Quickly. We must rouse everyone."

Eddie and Timothy and the elder Meades all work very hard each day, so it is no wonder that they sleep deeply and had been unaware of the fire. But within moments the house was filled with light and commotion.

"Grab all the buckets," Mr. Meade called to his family as he tucked his nightshirt into his trousers. In a moment Eddie and Timothy rushed out to the barn and returned with the milk pails. I didn't know what they were for, but I carried a huge soup pot that Mrs. Meade thrust into my arms. And now that I know how to walk in the dark, I quickly followed the Meade family across the meadow.

The smell of smoke grew stronger and stronger as we walked.

"It's the Turners' barn," shouted Mr. Meade. He had run way ahead of the rest of us in the direction of the fire. "Thank God their house is not attached to it!"

We all were out of breath as we approached. There were huge flames every-where. I could hear the crackling sound of burning wood and the anguished voices of people and the cries of animals too. It was a horrible and frightening sight, and I began to tremble.

"Are the animals out?" shouted Mrs. Meade above the noises.

Mr. Meade disappeared inside the burning barn.

"Oh, no," shouted Nell, sobbing. "He'll be killed by the fire. I know it!"

"Shhh," Emma said, putting her arms around her sister and trying to comfort her.

But by the light of the flames I could see the fear on her face too.

Then, miraculously, covered with soot, Mr. Meade came out of the barn, leading a horse that seemed wild with fear.

I saw other horses and cows being shooed to a far-off field. I wondered if any more animals were still inside the burning barn.

We were not the only people roused from our beds. Before long the Bentley family was there too and several other people I had not met before. By the light of the flames I quickly saw why I was carrying that big soup pot. We all joined the Turners, who, like us, were still wearing nightgowns and nightshirts. We stood in a line that went from the Turners' well to the barn. The soup pot and the milk pails, and all manner of other vessels, were filled with water and passed hand over hand toward the barn. By now the flames seemed to have encompassed the entire building. And even though I was many, many yards away, I could feel the heat of the fire as I stood passing each pail of water that was thrust into my hands. Smoke filled my lungs, and the crackling of the fire had a terrible sound.

It was useless. Even working as carefully as possible, as much water splashed out of each bucket as made it to the barn. I feared for the safety of Mr. Meade and his sons. They stood closest to the fire. Suppose some of the burning wooden beams fell on them! Somehow, in the midst of my concern about the Meade men and the Turner barn, my mind flew to Ruthi working on the top floor of the shirt factory. I have seen where she works. The windows are nailed shut. Suppose there was a fire while she was working inside. How could she get out? I don't know why I had that thought just then. But the possibility of my sister's being in such a horrible danger made me shudder, and I slopped more water than ever onto myself and the ground.

"Watch what you're doing," a voice yelled at me.

I grabbed the next pail that came toward me and the next and the next.

Eventually, when we all were so exhausted that I didn't think we could possibly pass another bucket, the fire was extinguished. But it was not because we had successfully doused it with the water. Rather, it had burned itself out. The barn was nothing more than a collection of blackened timbers, and the hay was totally consumed by the flames.

Mr. Meade and his sons remained behind with some of their other neighbors to soak the ground around the barn area. "They must watch that the fire doesn't start up elsewhere," Mrs. Meade explained to me as we walked back wet, sooty, and worn-out from our fire-fighting efforts. "Sometimes plant roots are on fire and the burning continues unseen underground. So the danger of fire won't be over until the next good rainstorm."

"How did the fire start?" I asked.

"Maybe someone knocked over a kerosene lamp," suggested Emma.

"There are many ways for a fire to begin," said Mrs. Meade. "A burning cigarette, a kerosene lamp, a bolt of lightning. One must always be on guard. Fire is a terrible disaster for a farmer."

"Fire is terrible for everyone," I said. "We have fires in New York City, but the fire department sends trucks loaded with water to help put them out. Our tenement has special iron steps so that people can climb downstairs and be rescued if there is a fire." Was there a fire escape at Ruthi's factory? I couldn't remember.

"There is a fire department here too," said Nell. "But they don't know when we have a fire so far from the center of town. Someday everyone will have telephones and be able to notify the firefighters. Then they could get here quickly. I heard Papa say it."

"Yes," said her mother. "And the sooner the better. You can't keep trouble from coming, but you don't have to give it a chair to sit in."

"I heard Mr. Turner say he was relieved that all his livestock was saved," said Emma consolingly.

"True. But his cows won't give milk anymore this summer," said Mrs. Meade. "A fright like this will dry them up."

"And poor Mr. Turner lost his barn," I added.

"They say it makes a difference whose cow is in the well," said Mrs. Meade, "but around here we all help one another rebuild after a disaster like this. It could happen to any of us anytime. We all know that. If we didn't help one another, we couldn't survive."

As we walked back toward the house, the sky was already getting light and birds were beginning to sing their morning songs. But I still kept thinking about the fire. The Meades were so rich compared with Ruthi and me. They had a big house, land, and plenty of food. But now I realized that they had plenty of worries too. If the weather wasn't good, their crops could fail. Sickness could attack them at any time, just as it attacked people in the city. If there was a fire, they could lose everything in an hour.

Suddenly the damaged library book seemed a very minor problem. No one's life was endangered by a soiled volume. I still knew that I had to resolve what I would do about it, but it no longer weighed on me so heavily.

I walked toward Emma and took her hand. "I forgive you for what happened to the library book," I said softly. "I'm sorry I was angry with you."

Emma looked at me and then squeezed my fingers. "Dossi," she said, "I've thought of a way that we can make money. Enough money to buy a new book."

My heart filled with happiness. But whether it was because Emma had a plan or because it was the first time she called me Dossi I cannot say.

August 10, 1910

*H*ere is Emma's plan: We're going to pick wild blackberries and sell them to the general store. Emma says we can get ten cents a quart. If we both pick and Nell helps too, before long we'll earn enough money to pay for the ruined library book.

I'm eager to begin picking. Unfortunately it began to rain an hour after Emma revealed her plan. The rain was a blessing, according to Mrs. Meade. It meant that any smoldering plant roots near the Turner barn would certainly be extinguished.

"The rain's important for growing berries too," Emma said to console me.

But if it doesn't stop raining, we can't go picking. Wet berries quickly turn moldy, according to Emma.

Anyhow, since I couldn't pick berries, I decided this was a good day to visit Wilson Bentley. When I told Mrs. Meade that he'd invited me to see his photographs, she smiled and nodded.

"Uncle Willie is as proud as a dog with two tails with those pictures he's taken," she told me. "And they *are* amazing. We've all seen them about a hundred times already. You go ahead, and the girls will help me with the canning."

"Can't I go with Dossi?" begged Nell.

"You've seen the pictures before, and you'll see them again," her mother said. "I need your help chopping vegetables this morning."

So I went off alone in the rain with an old shawl of Mrs. Meade's over my head for protection. I was a bit shy of funny little Uncle Willie and I wished that Nell were along for company. She is never at a loss for words. It seemed to me it would be helpful to have her standing nearby.

As it turned out, however, quiet Wilson Bentley becomes very excited when he starts talking about his snowflake photographs. His blue eyes shone intently, and he lectured me with great passion about the marvels of nature.

"Uncle Willie," I asked, "did you study about all this at college?"

"I never went to any classes beyond the local school," he said. "I'm sorry now. There is so much I'll never know, though I read and read what others have written."

"I think you must know as much as a college professor," I said, looking at picture after picture. Before me were the most amazing six-pointed images, each one delicate, each one just as beautiful as the one I'd admired a moment before. Perhaps strangest of all was the knowledge that I was looking at photographs of *snowflakes*.

"Notice that no two are the same," said Uncle Willie. "Though they exist side by side, each is different and unique. Just like human beings."

He was right. I'd never thought of it that way. But it's true. No two people are ever exactly alike, even two sisters like Ruthi and me or Emma and Nell. No wonder it has taken time for me to feel comfortable with Emma and the whole Meade family. We are so different. Yet as I get to know them better, I can see that we are also very much the same.

I looked down at the snowflake photographs again. "These are all so beautiful," I said. "They should be in a book so everyone could see all these pictures."

"Perhaps someday that will come to pass. It's one of my dreams," Uncle Willie said hopefully. "In the meantime, however, I've written a few articles about what I've learned. I'm very pleased to know that my words have been published and can be read by people I'll never meet. Why, do you know the journals that printed my pieces are on file in big public and university libraries all over the country? Imagine that!"

"They're completing work on an enormous library in New York City," I told him, just as I had told Emma and Nell. "It's all made of marble, and it will be a research library for scholars and ordinary citizens to use. I'm sure your articles will be in there too."

"When the library opens, you must go and check," Uncle Willie told me. Then he said, "Do you know that your new library used to be in Vermont?"

"Used to be in Vermont?" I repeated.

"Yes indeed. Every piece of marble that was used to build that grand New York library came from the quarries here in Vermont. From Dorset, Vermont, to be exact. I read all about it in the newspaper."

"Really?" I asked.

He nodded.

"What an amazing coincidence," I told him. "It's funny to think that even before I ever set foot in Vermont, I'd seen a chunk of the state that had come to settle in New York City."

He smiled at my words. "Vermont is a beautiful place," he said. "Someday you must come visit us in the winter, when it's painted white with frost and snow. I feel very blessed to have had the good fortune of being born right here, in Jericho, in the very house where I still live. To me it is the most beautiful place on earth. Perhaps that's why I've never traveled very far from here. But sometimes I think I should have gone off to college."

"You could still go," I suggested.

"No," he said. "I'm not a young man anymore. There's too much work for me to do right here. There are thousands of pictures for me still to take. Not just snowflakes, but ice crystals and dewdrops too. Each tells us a story, don't you know?"

I nodded. It seemed funny to be standing in my damp clothing in the wooden shed, where Uncle Willie does his work, and listening to him lecture. But the words he said are still echoing in my head.

Before I left, he gave me a gift. "Pick one for yourself," he offered, pointing to the stack of photographs on the table.

It wasn't easy. Each snowflake seemed more beautiful than the one before.

"Sometimes in life one just has to act," said

Uncle Willie when I seemed unable to make a decision.

"You're right," I agreed, and pointed to the snowflake closest at hand.

"It's yours!" he said. He took out his pen and signed his name and the date on the back of the photograph. Then he wrapped my picture in several sheets of old newspaper to protect it, even though the rain seemed to be letting up.

"Thank you," I said to the small man. "I'll never forget what you've shown and told me."

"And I'll never forget your kind interest and your smile, my dear," he said as I walked out the door.

It's easy to see why the townspeople call him Snowflake Bentley. But now that I've spoken with him at length, I realize that the name does not mock him but is given in love.

Soon it will be suppertime. Since the rain continued off and on all day, Mr. Meade and his sons went fishing. Mrs. Meade has prepared the trout they caught for our meal. Now, however, the rain seems to have really stopped. If tomorrow is clear, Emma and Nell and I will begin picking berries. As I'm going home in just a few more days, we haven't much time to earn money. In the meantime I've put the damaged library book under the mattress of my bed. Perhaps the pressure of my body will flatten the pages and improve the appearance of the book, although I tend to doubt it.

August 11, 1910

*H*urrah! The sun was shining when I woke this morning. Emma, Nell, and I ate breakfast quickly, and I helped them both perform their morning chores. As we rushed about, Mrs. Meade said, "Goodness, the three of you are as busy as butter on a hot griddle." She knew we were eager to earn some money, but she still didn't know why. Emma confessed to me that she has a reputation for being careless with things around the house. She didn't want her mother to learn of another example of that sort of behavior on her part. Finally everything that needed doing was done and we could set off to pick blackberries.

We walked up the hill to the edge of the Meade property. There are high bushes and a stand of trees. "Watch your step," Emma warned me. "It doesn't matter if you trip now, but you won't want to fall when you have a full basket."

The blackberries grow on prickly branches. I could feel the brambles through my long sleeves, but I didn't complain. Each berry brought us closer to our goal.

"Nell, stop eating!" Emma ordered when she saw what her sister was doing.

"We always eat when we pick," Nell protested.

"Not this year. In the past we were picking so Mama could make a pie. It didn't matter if the berries got inside our stomach straight from the bush or cooked in our dessert. These berries aren't meant for us to eat."

"Will Eddie and Timothy be disappointed not to have blackberry pie?" I asked.

"Mama can make an apple cobbler instead. The apples will be ripe any day, and that's their real favorite," Emma said.

The sun beat down on our heads, and my nose tickled from the scent of wildflowers. Bees buzzed nearby, and mosquitoes too. Sometimes I would see half a dozen berries growing close together. Other times I had to stand on my toes and stretch to reach just one tiny black fruit. The berries were small, and it took a long time to fill a single quart.

After a while Nell grew tired and stopped picking. She lay on the grass watching us. I wanted to join her, but I knew I couldn't stop. Otherwise I'd never have enough berries to earn the money. Gradually the basket grew heavier on my arm.

"How much do we have now?" I asked.

Emma examined the contents of my basket. "If we're lucky, the berries that the three of us have picked will fill three quarts."

"Three quarts?" I said. "That's only thirty cents. I need a dollar and a half to pay for the book. The price is printed right on the jacket.

Do you think we're going to earn enough money this way?"

"Mama says take care of the dimes and the dollars will take care of themselves," said Nell.

I hoped that Mrs. Meade was right about that.

"Let's take a rest," Emma suggested. From her pocket she removed a cloth that held three biscuits her mother had given us as a treat.

We sat nibbling our biscuits to make them last longer. It felt good to sit after standing for so long.

"I'll miss you when you return home," Emma said shyly.

"I'll miss you too," I responded at once, and I really meant it. These past couple of days, since the fire, I've felt truly at ease with the Meades. They've stopped treating me as a guest and more like part of the family. "You didn't like me very much at first, did you?" I asked Emma.

"That's because she didn't know how nice you are!" Nell exclaimed. "That's why she sometimes acted as cross as a bear with a sore head. But I liked you the moment you got off the train."

"Hush, Nell," said Emma with embarrassment. She blushed and looked down at the ground. "Having you come was Mama's idea," she explained. "Uncle Willie went about speaking to all the neighbors. He said we should invite a city child to have a good summer here in the country. He won Mama over with his arguments, and she told Papa that if the summer visitor was a boy, he could help out on the farm. So imagine our surprise when we got a letter from the Fresh Air Fund saying they were sending a girl here."

"Papa didn't care," said Nell. "He said right away that girls need country air just as much as boys. He said we could learn about city life from you."

"Anyhow, you're so different from Mary Wells, who stayed with the Bentleys, that I didn't know what to make of you," said Emma, going on. "Mary Wells giggled all the time. She told us fantastic stories about living in a mansion and having servants to take care of all her needs."

"Mary Wells sounds like a good storyteller," I said. "People who live in mansions and have servants don't need charity holidays in the country."

"I didn't think of that," said Emma. "Her stories were so good that we all liked to listen. She told us about the parties she went to and all the beautiful clothing and jewelry that she had at home. She said she'd gone riding in automobiles more times than she could remember. None of us has ever been in a motorcar."

Poor Mary, I thought. Creating fantasies to impress her new friends.

"I liked Mary Wells," said Emma. "Even though she held her nose whenever she went into the barn, she seemed funny, and she made me laugh. But now I like you better. You may not even be Christian, but somehow you seem just like us. You help with the chores, you're willing to learn new things, and you're honest."

"You helped save the Turners' animals!"

Nell shouted out. "I heard Mr. Turner tell Papa that if he and Eddie and Timothy hadn't arrived when they did, he'd never have managed to get the horses and cows out of the barn. And Papa said, 'It's our city visitor you should be thanking. She woke us all.'"

I looked at Nell with amazement. I didn't know that Mr. Meade thought I was responsible for such a good deed.

"Do you remember when you asked if you could come and visit me in New York City?" I asked Emma.

She nodded her head.

"The reason I didn't agree at once is that we live so poorly compared with your family. But now my sister has written that she's going to get married. Soon we'll be living in a new tenement and have more space." I thought for a moment. Even *more space* in the city would seem congested to someone brought up in these wide-open spaces. Nevertheless, I went ahead. "Perhaps it will be possible for you to come after all. I should like it very much."

"It was wrong of me to ask you," said

Emma. "Come," she said, standing up and brushing off her skirt. "Enough resting. Let's walk over to the spring and get a drink of water before we go back to picking."

I jumped up and took both of Emma's hands. "It's terrible that my library book got ruined, but it's fun to pick berries with you."

"I feel just awful about the book. I'm glad you've forgiven me for leaving it out in the rain. And I think this dilemma about replacing the book has taught me a better lesson than all the words that Mama said on the subject. I know I won't act so carelessly in the future."

"I'm sure you won't," I assured Emma. "It was a good story, wasn't it?" I asked her. What with my concern about the book, we'd never talked about its contents.

"I loved it," Emma agreed. "Remember the part when Anne dyes her hair and it turns green?"

"Green?" shrieked Nell. "Green hair?"

"Yes," her sister told her. "She had beautiful red hair, just like Dossi, but she wanted to change the color."

We all laughed together at the thought of someone with green hair. And I was flattered that Emma had called my hair beautiful.

We continued picking berries until we heard the faint ring of the cowbell that Mrs. Meade uses to call her family back home. I was very hot and very tired, so I was glad that it was lunchtime. But it was a profitable morning.

August 12, 1910

*L*ast night Mrs. Meade made pancakes for supper. We ate them with maple syrup. It was the most delicious thing I ever tasted. Mrs. Meade laughed. She says everything of hers that I eat I claim is *the most delicious*. I read about maple syrup in our geography book at school, but it was the first time I ever tasted it.

"It's hard to believe that it pours out of the tree trunks in the spring," I marveled as I poured syrup on a second helping of pancakes.

"Not exactly pours out," Timothy corrected

me. "The sap comes out, but there's still a tremendous amount of work before we have syrup like this."

The pancakes reminded me a little of the blintzes that Mrs. Aronson sometimes makes. Mama used to make blintzes too.

"Do you ever cook blintzes?" I asked Mrs. Meade.

"Blintzes?" Nell giggled. "What a funny word! Blintzes. Blintzes," she repeated.

Mrs. Meade shook her head. "What is it?" she wanted to know.

I explained that it's a very thin pancake onto which cheese or fruit is placed, and then it's rolled up. "If you added more milk and eggs to your batter, you could do the same thing here. And you have such delicious things to use as filling," I said, thinking of the jars of preserved fruit in the cellar and the fresh farmer's cheese that Mrs. Meade made from their own milk.

"Let's try it!" said Emma. "If it's good, we could bring blintzes to the next church supper."

Right away Nell began explaining to me that once a month the members of their church prepare a meal. Everyone brings a food item to share with the others. "Mama always brings a chicken potpie. It would be a big surprise to have something new and different to bring."

"It's too bad the next church supper is after you are gone," said Emma.

It is too bad. Even though I didn't want to go to their religious services, it might have been fun to meet all the people at the church supper. "I know many good recipes," I offered. "My mother made stuffed cabbage. I used to help her." It was funny how that memory suddenly returned to me. I had not thought about stuffed cabbage in a long, long time.

"Stuffed pancakes, stuffed cabbage," said Mrs. Meade, smiling. "You do have some unusual ideas."

"We have a hundred heads of cabbage out in the garden," said Timothy, "and there's a limit to the amount of slaw one family can consume happily."

"You're leaving in a few days," said Mrs. Meade, turning to me. "I guess you must begin giving me cooking lessons at once."

"Oh, no," I said. "You're such a good cook."

"Even a good cook, like a young dog, can learn some new tricks," said Mrs. Meade, smiling at me.

So this morning, before I went off berry picking with the girls, I showed Mrs. Meade how Mama used to boil the cabbage leaves to make them soft. Then she filled them with a mixture of chopped meat and onions.

After the "lesson" Emma, Nell, and I picked another two quarts of berries. I don't think there's another berry left in the whole area. And that's a good thing. I'm tired of all that picking. I don't want to see another berry bush!

All together we had about seven quarts. Seventy cents' worth, we thought. Not enough money for my needs, but it was a start.

Mr. Meade was going into town on some errands, so he hitched up Dandy to the wagon and drove us to the general store. I don't know how we would have been able to walk the distance, without spilling all our berries, if he hadn't given us the ride.

There was bad news at the store. Emma remembered that Mr. Clark sells berries each year. What she hadn't taken into account is that he buys them for less than the ten cents he sells them for. He offered us seven cents a quart. Seven times seven is only forty-nine.

"Oh, no," moaned Emma. "We need more money than that."

I didn't say a word. But I felt terrible. Forty-nine cents was less than a third of the amount of money I needed. "Tell you what," said Mr. Clark, looking at Emma's and Nell's and my disappointed faces. "I'll give you fifty cents. But not a penny more. And don't tell anyone about it. I can't afford to give my money away."

I swallowed hard and looked at Emma. She looked at me.

"Fifty cents is a lot of money," said Nell. For a moment she forgot we needed the money to buy a new book. "You could buy two pounds of candy or eight pounds of gingersnaps with that much money." She looked around the store at the different items and their prices. "You could get three pounds of English tea or two tins of talcum powder."

I think Nell must be a good arithmetic student, she was so quick to figure out all the purchases we could make. I looked at Emma, and despite my concern about the money, I began to smile. "Maybe if I brought the librarian some tea or some talcum powder, she would overlook the condition of the book."

"Eight pounds of gingersnaps would change anyone's opinion," Emma said. "It will also give them an upset stomach." She began to smile too.

Of course we didn't buy any of those items. But we accepted Mr. Clark's offer and turned over our seven quarts of blackberries and received two worn quarters in exchange.

As we rode home, Emma said, "I have twenty cents in my handkerchief box. I will give it to you."

"I have five cents," said Nell. "You could have that."

"I still have twenty-five cents from my sister," I said. The rest of my money had been spent on lemon drops and licorice whips, which I bought for Emma and Nell and myself whenever we walked into town. I had planned to use the rest to buy a gift to take home to Ruthi.

"Why do you girls need money?" asked Mr. Meade, overhearing our comments.

"Dossi needs to replace her library book. It was ruined when I left it out in the rain," Emma admitted to her father.

"How much more money do you need?" Mr. Meade wanted to know.

"Fifty cents," said Nell. She *was* good in arithmetic.

Mr. Meade turned to me. "Don't worry about the money," he said. "Mr. Turner was asking me how he could reward you for rousing us the night of the fire. Now I know the answer."

I looked at him with surprise.

"Hurrah!" shouted Nell. "Now if we pick more berries, we can have a pie after all."

I rubbed together the two quarters that I was holding in my fist. The backs of both my hands were covered with scratches that I got berry picking. But those scratches would soon be healed, and the book would be paid for.

"I'll help you pick," I promised Nell.

August 15, 1910

My valise is almost packed. I woke early this morning, even before the sky grew light. This is my last morning here in Jericho, and in a few hours I'll be back aboard the train, going home. The train strike has been settled, so my ride to New York City should take less time than my trip here.

It's strange that I feel sad to be leaving when just two weeks ago I was so reluctant to come. But so much has happened in fourteen days. I've seen and done so many new things. Yesterday I even milked a cow!

Timothy had been teasing me about milking. He said if I didn't do it, they wouldn't permit me to return home. Twice I went to the barn during the evening milking period to watch. I like looking at Timothy when he's busy and not looking at me. But both times I refused his offer of a lesson in cow milking.

I think what scared me most was the idea of *sitting down* to milk a cow. Cows are so big. If I could face them standing up, at least I'd be able to run out of the barn quickly if need be. The thought of sitting next to one of those huge creatures and pulling at the udders was not one that appealed to me at all.

So each time I stood back and watched as Eddie and Timothy did the milking. They sat and calmly squeezed the milk from the cow with the same ease with which I work the water pump in the Meade kitchen. If one of the cows swung her tail and hit them in the head, they merely laughed.

"You'd swing your tail too, if you had one, Red," Timothy said when I commented on it. "In fact, I envy the cows. A tail would be very useful for shooing off the flies," he said.

Yesterday was Sunday again. On the Christian Sabbath the family does as little work as possible. But certain chores must be performed daily. In the afternoon Mrs. Meade and Emma and Nell sent me out of the kitchen. I guessed they were preparing a special supper to mark my departure. I walked around the yard, silently bidding good-bye to the woodpile, the vegetable garden, the pig, the chickens, and even Dandy, the horse, although I'll see him again when he brings me to the train. Finally I walked to the barn. Eddie and Timothy were inside milking the cows.

I stood in the doorway watching. One of the cats ran past me suddenly and made me jump.

"Come on in," called Eddie.

"Hey, Red, won't you try milking at least once?" asked Timothy.

Bravely I walked toward the stall where he was sitting.

"Look," he said. "I just pull on one udder with my right hand and another with my left. Gently but firmly."

As he spoke, the milk squirted down into

the pail. When he did it, the task seemed so simple and easy. I looked at the white, foamy liquid. What magic! Later I would drink it or Mrs. Meade would use it in her cooking.

"Old Bettie is the gentlest of our cows," said Timothy. He pushed back his milking stool and stood up.

I sat down and reached out my hands and cautiously took hold of two of the udders. "Like this?" I asked.

"Pull harder," he said when nothing happened. "You won't hurt her. She's used to it." He squatted down beside me and was so close that I could feel the warmth of his body and smell his sweat and the soap with which he had recently washed himself. He put his hands over mine and squeezed first one and then the other. Milk spurted into the pail.

"Now do it alone," he instructed as he removed his hands from mine. But he remained squatting next to me.

I took a deep breath, clenched down on my teeth, and took a firmer grip on Bettie's udders. Amazingly a bit of milk dripped down into the pail. I looked at Timothy proudly.

"You're doing it," he said. He patted me encouragingly on the back.

I pulled again and again. More milk came out. In fact, it actually squirted down, just the way it did when Eddie and Timothy did the milking.

"I knew it," said Timothy. "You're a natural. Maybe you'd better not go home tomorrow. We can use you to help out here in the barn," he teased.

I blushed at his words. I like Timothy, and I'll miss him when I'm home.

When I stood up, my arms ached from the tension with which I'd held them during the past few minutes. "I won't take your job away," I said.

"Good work," Eddie called out to me. He had moved on and milked two cows while I had been doing my small performance.

I almost danced out of the barn. Imagine. I'd milked a cow. Wait till I tell Ruthi and Mimi. Would they or anyone else on Essex Street ever believe a thing like that?

The supper was lovely. Mrs. Meade had cooked all the things she remembered I especially liked. We had fried fish with potatoes, applesauce, sliced tomatoes, and corn on the cob. For a sweet at the end of the meal she served a wonderful golden brown cake.

"Do you know what this is?" she asked as she cut me a large slice.

"Cake?"

"This isn't just any cake. The recipe for this cake comes straight from the Old Testament," she said proudly.

"There're no cooking recipes in there," I said, wondering what sort of joke she was making.

"Yes indeed," she insisted, and everyone else agreed with her. Later, when the meal was over, she showed me a paper on which she had written down the cooking instructions. I still couldn't believe her. So Mr. Meade went and brought the huge family Bible. I carefully turned the pages and looked up every reference. Sure enough, each of the ingredients is listed there. I copied it to show Ruthi. Maybe after she is Mrs. Reisman, she'll want to make this cake for Meyer.

Mrs. Meade gave me presents to take

home. A tin of maple syrup and a jar of her strawberry preserves. I know Ruthi will enjoy them too.

"I wish I had something to give you in return," I said.

"But you have given us many things," said Mrs. Meade.

"No, I haven't."

"You certainly have! Your appreciation for all we have has made Emma and Nell more aware of their good fortune. And I for one am pleased to have finally gotten to know a Hebrew person. You may have some different customs, but deep down we're all the same. You're no different from us than our brown Jersey cows are from the Turners' black-and-white Holsteins."

"Mama," protested Emma, "you can't compare Dossi to a cow!"

"Mooo," I said, throwing my arms around first Mrs. Meade and then Emma and Nell in turn. What fine people they all are. I would've liked to give a hug to Timothy also, but I felt too shy. Instead I just smiled at all the men in the Meade family.

Suddenly I realized that there was something I could give them. "Just a moment," I cried out, and ran up the stairs to my attic room. I took the copy of *Anne of Green Gables* from under my mattress. It still showed signs of the time it had spent out in the rain. But the pages were dry, and I could turn each of them. And the words and front illustration were there.

"I wish I had something new and beautiful to give you," I said, holding out the book. "But since I'm going to pay the library to buy a new copy, this one must belong to me. And so that means I can give it to you."

I handed the book to Emma.

"Oh, Dossi!" she exclaimed. "This is a wonderful gift. And do you know what? Now I can finally finish reading the story."

"That book will remind you not to be so careless," said her mother, who had finally learned the truth about the poor book.

"No. It'll remind you of the fun we had picking berries," I corrected.

"I'll read it aloud to everyone during the

winter," Emma promised. "You'll all laugh when you hear the story."

"We'll laugh, and we'll think of you," Nell promised me.

"For once our Nell is speaking some sense," said Mrs. Meade.

Now I think I hear Emma and Nell getting dressed in their room. So I'll finish this page and close my ink bottle really tightly once more. I'll wrap it in my underclothes, just as I did when I packed to come here. The next time I write, I'll be back on Essex Street. I'm eager to see Ruthi again and to greet my new brother-to-be. But I know I'll miss the Meades and the town of Jericho.

Emma says that she hopes I can return next summer for another visit. That would be wonderful! In the meantime, however, we've promised that we'll write letters to each other.

"Write one to me!" Nell pleaded. I remember that she said she's never received a letter. I'll be pleased to be the first to send one to her.

I know that I'll often turn back the pages of this diary and reread about all that happened to me during August 1910. And I'll often look at the special pages in my autograph album where all my new friends have inscribed their names. When school opens in September, I must be sure to tell Miss Blythe that I've filled so many pages in the book she gave me. Won't she be amazed?

From My Autograph Album

You are always welcome in our home.
            Sincerely, Ida Meade

～～～～～～～～～～～～～～～～～～～～～～～～

Edward Meade, Sr.

～～～～～～～～～～～～～～～～～～～～～～～～

Edward Meade, Jr.

～～～～～～～～～～～～～～～～～～～～～～～～

Timothy Meade

～～～～～～～～～～～～～～～～～～～～～～～～

Dear Dossi;
I will miss you. Come back to Jericho.
                        Nell

～～～～～～～～～～～～～～～～～～～～～～～～

Dearest Dossi,
    I will always remember you and the summer
of 1910. Please come back in 1911, 1912, 1913. . . .
You have become my very special friend.
                Your true friend, Emma Meade

May you be like the snowflakes that fall from heaven: discover your unique qualities.

The snowflakes melt and disappear. The memory of your visit will remain with all who crossed paths with you this summer.

Sincerely, Wilson Alwyn Bentley

August 14, 1910

Biblical Fruit Cake

1 cup	Genesis, Chapter 18, Verse 8 (butter)
1 cup	Psalms, Chapter 19, Verse 10 (sugar)
4 whole	Jeremiah, Chapter 17, Verse 11 (eggs)
2 cups	Kings I, Chapter 4, Verse 22 (flour)
1½ cups	Samuel I, Chapter 30, Verse 12 (raisins)
1½ cups	Song of Solomon, Chapter 7, Verse 7 (dates)
1 cup	Numbers, Chapter 17, Verse 8 (almonds)
½ cup	Genesis, Chapter 24, Verse 17 (water)
2 teaspoons	Exodus, Chapter 16, Verse 31 (honey)
1 teaspoon	Amos, Chapter 4, Verse 5 (baking powder)
Pinch	Leviticus, Chapter 2, Verse 13 (salt)

Season to taste according to Chronicles II, Chapter 9, Verse 9 (cinnamon, ginger, nutmeg).

Take the first three ingredients and follow Solomon's advice, as noted in Proverbs, Chapter 23, Verses 13–14 (beat well).

Chop almonds and dates and add together with the other ingredients. Mix thoroughly. Pour batter into a floured and buttered tube pan with a removable bottom.

Bake at 350 degrees for 60 minutes. Test with a toothpick to be sure cake batter has fully cooked. Cool in pan before removing.

This cake does not need frosting. However, if you sprinkle confectioner's sugar through a strainer, it will look as if snowflakes have fallen on the cake.

Mount Lebanon Academy
P.O. Box 10357
Pittsburgh, PA 15234

Author's Note

This is a work of fiction. The Rabinowitz sisters and the Meade family exist only in my imagination. However, much of their story is based on fact. The Fresh Air Fund was established in 1877 and still exists. Its goal is to provide free two-week summer vacations in the country for disadvantaged city children. Well over a million young people have benefited from this program over the years.

I did not make up Wilson Alwyn Bentley. He lived in Jericho, Vermont, from 1865 to 1931. He did indeed photograph snowflakes and was the first to discover that no two flakes are the same. Essays of his were published in various journals, and in 1931, shortly before his death, a volume of his snowflake pictures was published by the American Meteorological Society. One of these photographs is reprinted in this book with the permission of the Jericho Historical Society.

During Bentley's lifetime, he was an active supporter of the Fresh Air Fund. Though he never married, he was close to his brother's family, made up of eight nieces and nephews, all of whom had names beginning with the letter *A*. He loved music and frequently entertained his family and neighbors by playing piano for them.

The Triangle Shirtwaist Factory, where Ruthi is employed, really existed. It was the site of a devastating fire in March 1911. As an author of fiction I had the power to set my story in 1910 and to tell my readers that Ruthi would be married within a few months and leave her job. In that way I could at least save *her* life, if not the lives of the 146 women who died in the blaze the following spring.

While researching information for this book, I read back issues of the *Brattleboro Reformer* and the *Rutland Herald* newspapers on microfilm. I traveled to Jericho, Vermont, and visited the Tenement Museum on New York's Lower East Side. I listened to Evelyn Keefe, of

Wilmington, Vermont, recount her memories of being a farmer's daughter in the early years of the twentieth century. The Brattleboro Museum and Art Center had an exhibit about farming in Vermont that I found helpful.

In addition, I read many books about this period and learned many interesting facts. Among them was my discovery that the elegant public library building at Forty-second Street and Fifth Avenue, completed in 1911 and in which I was once employed, was constructed entirely from Vermont marble.

The Fresh Air Fund vacations did and continue to do more than merely give a holiday to city children. They introduce children from two different environments to one another, and this leads to growth and understanding for visitors and hosts alike.